MIDLOTHIAN LIBRARY SERVICE

Please return/renew this item by the last date shown. To
renew please give your borrower number. Renewal may
be made in person, online, or by post, e-mail or phone.
www.midlothian.gov.uk/library

THE RAVELSTON AFFAIR

The Ravelston Affair

by

Elizabeth Harrison

Dales Large Print Books
Long Preston, North Yorkshire,
BD23 4ND, England.

British Library Cataloguing in Publication Data.

Harrison, Elizabeth
    The Ravelston affair.

        A catalogue record of this book is
        available from the British Library

        ISBN   978-1-84262-581-1 pbk

First published in Great Britain in 1967
by Ward Lock & Co. Ltd.

Cover illustration by arrangement with
P.W.A. International Ltd.

The moral right of the author has been asserted

Published in Large Print 2008 by arrangement with
Elizabeth Harrison, care of Watson, Little Ltd.

Dales Large Print is an imprint of Library Magna Books Ltd.

Printed and bound in Great Britain by
T.J. (International) Ltd., Cornwall, PL28 8RW

I

As soon as Rodney Ravelston could find a free day, he travelled down to Brookhampton to see his cousin Hugh. He did so with dread. He had been away for three years, including almost a year in the United States, lecturing, between the two periods at the base in the Antarctic. The accounts he had heard of Hugh were depressing. He was afraid of what he would find.

Rodney had always felt responsible for Hugh. He was convinced that if he had been in the country at the time, he could have saved the situation. Hugh would still be in London, at the Central, instead of down at Brookhampton.

But he had not been at home. Worse, he had remained unaware for months of the inexorable march of events. He and Hugh had never been good correspondents, no one had told him what was happening. His own family, he was to discover later, had been forbidden to mention the affair to him.

Sir Donald Ravelston was the head of the family. In his eighties, pig-headed and obstinate, he had decided that Rodney was not to be bothered with Hugh's troubles. He would only be worried, he had declared, and there was nothing he could do. The family, though they had argued a little, had obeyed him, as they invariably did. They were all afraid of the old man. None of them told Rodney what had happened, and it was left to him to find out, six months later, in a letter from a colleague at the Central London Hospital, where he worked in the research laboratories when he was at home. *Nothing much has occurred here since the downfall of your cousin H.D.R. – that shook the place almost to the foundations, I can tell you. A Ravelston does not bite the dust every day. Personally, I was sorry for the young idiot. There's no doubt, though, a great many little minds were charmed to see the child of privilege reduced – if you will forgive the mixed metaphor – to the ranks. The G.O.M. himself* (to his family Sir Donald Ravelston was the old man. To the hospital, where he had been Professor of Medicine for thirty years, until his belated retirement ten years earlier, he had long been very grand indeed – hence, naturally, the G.O.M.) *appeared in our midst, looking unutterably gloomy and full of hauteur, as usual. Enough to frighten poor young Hugh – who already had quite enough on his plate, one would have thought – into committing hara-kiri. What the G.O.M. said or did we none of us know, because nothing was ameliorated, no punches were pulled, young Hugh was duly cast to the lions, and the lions made a fine meal of him. There are those who assert that the Professor Emeritus played the stern role of a Roman father – or, strictly speaking, grandfather – and denounced the youngest Ravelston as clearly as any. Certainly he did nothing to save him.*

This was only too likely, Rodney recognised immediately. Sir Donald Ravelston had little time for his youngest grandson. Hugh had always been a disappointment to him. Useless to ask his grandfather what had happened, Rodney knew. He wrote to Emma, and elicited as much of the story as she had heard. It made miserable reading for him, and the slowness of the mails, his own inability to take a hand in the matter, increased his grief and frustration.

As soon as his grandfather discovered that the story was known to Rodney, he too wrote. Had Emma made it clear what was behind it all? Drunkenness and fast driving – and womanising. There had been two women mixed up in the affair, one of them a patient. The old man was shocked.

Rodney had written furiously back defending Hugh. He was no worse than any other young man. He had simply, it seemed, had appalling luck. Many young men drove fast cars. Many young men took beautiful girls to alcoholic parties. There, but for the Grace of God, go all of us, he argued.

Sir Donald Ravelston disagreed. He was

9

finished with Annabel's wretched boy. Let him go and join Annabel in her dubious continental haunts. 'I wash my hands of him.'

But Hugh had not gone to join Annabel. He had gone to Brookhampton, where he had been found a job, Emma reported, by Jock Calderwood, Ben Calderwood's father, who was the pathologist there.

Good, reliable old Ben, Rodney thought affectionately, trust him to have stayed on the job. In spite of his grandfather's forecasts, evidently Hugh had not been without supporters. He must have needed them. And when it came to it, there could have been little they could do to make life easier for him. It was Hugh who had to live it, day by day. Hugh who had faced the charge of manslaughter, who, after months of uncertainty, had appeared before the General Medical Council.

The Council had – its usual formula – directed that the name of Hugh Donald Ravelston be erased from the register. This was far worse than anyone had expected. At the Central they had been stunned. A Ravelston struck off.

Two camps immediately formed, for and against. But this made little difference to Hugh. He handed over his work and left the Central.

Now Rodney was going to meet him. Since his own return from the Antarctic, he had deliberately, with some difficulty, planned his affairs so that he could travel to Brookhampton before seeing them all at the Central. Here he would have had first-hand accounts of what had happened. But he had resolutely set his face against this. At least, he had determined, he would go down to see Hugh without being filled with the hospital gossip on his affairs.

So now he sat in the train, wondering what he was going to find, asking himself what these past three years would have done to Hugh.

Hugh had always been lighthearted, witty. This was what their grandfather had disliked. He considered him superficial and pleasure-seeking. The Ravelstons were serious. Hugh had Annabel's gaiety and charm, her effervescent high spirits, and it was true that he liked a good time. He was sociable, popular, sought after. He was excellent company, ready to make any party last till dawn. What had he made of life in Brookhampton, working as little more than a laboratory technician, doing routine chores? Even more to the point, what had life in Brookhampton made of him?

Rodney frowned. Brookhampton was not Siberia. If Hugh could not stand up to a few years of routine work in a provincial town, then he was as superficial as the old man said.

Arriving at Brookhampton station, Rodney asked the way to Malden Road, and was directed to take a bus, get off at the Odeon, and ask again. He did this, and was directed along a street of small shops – grocers, cleaners, chemist, shoe repairs, newsagents. The shops became smaller and meaner. Turn left and then right. Malden Road. So this was where Hugh lived. Rows of late Victorian terraced houses, two storey red brick, tiny front gardens with railings and privet hedges, staring across the narrow street at their mirror images. For all his conjectures, it was a shock to find that Hugh lived here. Rodney could not picture him at all in this environment. What did he do? How did he live in the midst of these houses, these people? He rang the bell of 35, Malden Road. A young woman answered, attractive and well-dressed. Looking past her into the strip of hall, seeing the highly-polished linoleum, he asked for Hugh.

'Oh, he's at the hospital tonight,' she said. 'He wont be back till late.'

'Oh,' Rodney said, surprised. This didn't sound too bad. Nor was the house as dreary as he had feared. The hall was neat, and brightly painted. He could hear the television – in fact, they were both shouting to be heard above it – but the place was not as grim as the picture he had built up in his mind, and the woman was far from being the classical landlady figure. 'Perhaps,' he said, 'I'll try and catch him there. Could you give me directions?'

She did this, and he walked back the way he had come, waited at the bus stop again. He had been foolish, he now realised, not to have telephoned Hugh first. He began to wish, too, that he had driven down. He had thought it would be easier and quicker by train, but he could have done with the car now. He waited ten minutes, his impatience growing, for a bus. When at last it came, his trip was brief, and he saw that he could have walked the distance in half the time he had spent at the bus stop. Suddenly he could hardly bear to wait even for a few minutes to see Hugh. Since he had spoken to the landlady, Hugh had sprung into reality for him, and all the nightmare imaginings seemed foolish.

So here he was at the hospital. A typical example of the converted workhouse, he noted, separated from the pavement by area railings, and looking out from ugly sash windows with frosted glass. But still at this time of the evening there was the unmistakable, and to Rodney homely, bustle of a busy general hospital. He went through swing doors into a wide square hall with black and white tiles, and painted notices with arrows hanging in mid-air over his head. *Outpatients, Ante-natal clinic, Wards A*

1-5, Steward, X-ray Department, Dispensary – they faded into the middle distance. Tiring of reading them, he turned to the hatch where the usual porter sat, at a switchboard, and asked for Hugh.

The man was as friendly as most hospital porters. 'Well, sir,' he said, 'I'll try him and see. But I don't suppose he'll be there now.' He manipulated the plugs, listened. 'No,' he said, 'I thought not. I'll ring him again, to make sure. No, he's not answering. If I were you, sir,' he paused, and his eyes momentarily bored into Rodney, with diagnostic concentration, 'yes,' he added, having satisfied himself, 'you'll be his brother, sir, I expect.'

'Cousin,' Rodney answered, with Ravelston accuracy.

'Cousin, is it, sir? Knew you was one of the family, anyway. Well, if I was you, sir, I'd just pop over to the Dog and Duck opposite, and I'd be willing to bet me last shilling you'll find his lordship havin' his supper, nice and cosy like.'

'Thanks very much, that's a great help,' Rodney said, though his heart sank. He told himself not to be ridiculous. As though the boy couldn't pop over to the pub for a pint, without being labelled an alcoholic. Squaring his shoulders, Rodney pushed through the doors of the Dog and Duck, and looked round.

He saw no sign of Hugh. There was a

crowd round the bar, several tables by the wall, and groups standing between the two, so that it took him a few minutes to be sure of this. Just as he was wondering what to do next, the barman caught his eye. An immediate light of recognition flickered across his face, and Rodney realised that once more the family likeness was coming to his aid. The barman said nothing. But he had an expressive face, and recognition was succeeded by enquiry, slightly quizzical enquiry, which Rodney reciprocated. The barman jerked his head back and sideways, and Rodney spotted a door at the side of the bar. He went through it.

This inner room was quiet, and evidently used by regulars. There were half a dozen tables, of which four were occupied. At one of them, beside a glowing coal fire, clearly, as the porter had foretold, 'having his supper nice and cosy like', his feet stretched out comfortably towards the blaze, sat Hugh.

No nightmare Hugh, this. Just Hugh as he had always been, wearing, at present, an expression of remote concentration as he read some journal. In front of him an innocuous pint of what looked like bitter, and bread and cheese. He had thinned down, certainly. His face was more angular, slightly beaky and saturnine. In fact, he had become unmistakably a Ravelston.

He looked up, as Rodney's shadow fell across the printed page, and his face was transformed. The remoteness vanished, to be superseded by instant delight and affection. For years Rodney had been warmed by this responsiveness of Hugh's, so unusual among the cold intellectual Ravelstons. Meeting Hugh again was just as it had always been – like entering a room where he was always sure of a welcome, and where no chill winds entered.

Yet of course this could not be so. For if ever anyone was out in the cold, Hugh Ravelston was.

II

A few years earlier, Hugh, the youngest of the brilliant and handsome Ravelstons, appeared – as the outpatient sister delighted to put it – to have the world at his feet.

Ravelston was a name to conjure with at the Central London Hospital, and had been for generations. Today there was old Sir Donald Ravelston, in his eighties, loaded with honours, a lifetime of distinguished service behind him. He had two sons, Archie, the father of Rodney and Don, and Andrew, Hugh's father. Both of them, needless to say,

Central men. Archie was a physiologist of standing, whose investigations into the properties of heart muscle twenty years earlier formed part of the basis of modern cardiology. He had qualified at the Central, had worked there for a number of years in the research laboratories, but had retired to the academic fastness of Cambridge a decade earlier. He was a contrast to old Sir Donald Ravelston, who, though always authoritarian, and latterly embittered, had been a great participant in the lives of those around him – family, staff, patients. Archie, though he had an impish sense of humour, which flashed unexpectedly and was the joy of those of his colleagues who did not happen to be on the receiving end, had always been of withdrawn temperament. At the Central they said he had married and produced his family in the periodic fits of absence of mind that alternated with hard work in the laboratory. He and his wife Jean were said to give their sons care and good food, but somewhat tepid affection.

Rodney, Archie's elder son, was as outstanding in his generation as his grandfather half a century previously. He was renowned, not only for the prizes he carried off – first the Kendall, then the Froome Medal, finally the Gurney-Higham, most coveted of distinctions, and previously awarded to both his father and grandfather – but also for his exploits on the rugger field and in off-shore racing. Cynics said that if he had not been brilliant but on the contrary hopelessly moronic, they would somehow have found a post for him at the Central as a result of his rugger playing alone.

Afloat, he was a helmsman of instinctive brilliance, and an unselfish and untiring crew member, whose courage and endurance were never in doubt.

All the Ravelstons were sailors. The children were afloat before they could walk, and learnt how to sail a dinghy before they could ride their first bicycles. Andrew, Hugh's father, had met his early death at sea, in a gale off Barfleur, when he had gone overboard to try and save his houseman, who had been crewing for him. They had both been lost, and Annabel, his wife, had never forgiven the sea for what it had done. She had forbidden their son ever to sail. But to forbid a Ravelston to sail was as effective as forbidding the tide to rise and fall.

Hugh had followed his cousins to the Central from Cambridge, and they said that this Ravelston, the youngest of the present generation, showed more promise than any of them since his grandfather. He was indubitably the best looking of a handsome family – lean, dark, blue-eyed, with the faint but unmistakable air of grandeur that was a Ravelston characteristic. All doors opened before him, and he had not been slow to pass through them. Gay, witty, effortlessly confident at work and play, it seemed, he had been surrounded by the pleasant aura of success.

Girls, of course, flocked round him. At the time of the crash he had been going around with Nicola Hanbury. Everyone assumed they would be married before the year was out.

Nicola was a charmer. She was the only girl Hugh had met who could be as enchanting as his mother, Annabel. Physically, though, Nicola was entirely different from Annabel. She was dark, in contrast to Annabel's fairness, with hair which reached her shoulders and which she arranged differently daily – often twice daily. Sometimes it hung straight and shoulder length, turning outwards at the ends, bell-like, swinging as she moved her small head on its slender neck, half-hiding her face as it fell from the centre parting across her velvety cheeks. At other times she would sweep it up round her head, in a dark swirling cloud, and the bones of her face suddenly grew fragile and delicate. Nicola had a wide mouth that crinkled into a fascinating smile over tiny even teeth, spaced out like a cat's. Her skin was pale and clear, transparent almost, and her eyes were green. They were always heavily made up, and her brows drawn to twirl fantastically upward. She was only a little over five feet in height, with narrow shoulders, tiny hands and feet. She was graceful in all her movements, stepped silently and lightly about, hardly, it seemed, disturbing even the dust as she went. In short, her fragility appeared to demand the gentlest handling only. All men longed to protect her, and Hugh was among them.

Nicola had been in and out of love before, but no one had ever stirred her as Hugh Ravelston did. She had seen him about the hospital – she was a medical secretary – long before he had noticed her. She had asked the other girls about him the first day she set eyes on him.

'Someone came into outpatients,' she said, 'when I was there looking for Dr Brogan. Tall and dark, quite young.'

'Who could it have been?' they wondered.

'Rather fabulous,' she added.

Light dawned. 'Oh, you must mean Hugh Ravelston. We all rather care for *him*. He's Vanstone's registrar, and fearfully brilliant, as well as utterly – well, you saw for yourself. M-m-hm.'

'He's just back from the Dinard race, of course – he crews in *Opening Snap*. They say he's nearly as good a helmsman as Rodney Ravelston – they're cousins, you know.'

She thought about him all afternoon. Afterwards, if she caught a glimpse of him as he walked across outpatients while she was there, disappeared round the corner of the corridor ahead of her, or she saw him entering a room in the distance, a glow came over her day.

Nicola was surrounded by men anxious to take her out. Those she favoured were either entertaining, good-looking or moneyed, for she could have her pick. But when Hugh Ravelston was about they might not have existed, as far as she was concerned. From the moment that she saw him, she knew that he would be the love of her life.

It was some time before he noticed her. He was studying hard for the Membership, and he already had a number of girl-friends, perhaps the foremost among them being Angela Carlton. Nicola had competition.

Angela Carlton was a beautiful strange creature, angular, almost emaciated, with hollow eyes and long limbs. People who disliked her called her 'the clothes horse'. Certainly she wore her striking clothes with an air, and she had the abnormal proportions of a model girl. She was known to be temperamentally difficult. Hugh in fact never particularly liked her, but she fascinated him with her beauty. Angela was one of those who could make hearts stand still with the haunting loveliness of a gesture, a movement, a turn of the head. He knew, too, that when they went out together they made a dramatic couple, and he enjoyed causing a stir, seeing heads turn. He seldom saw Angela alone. When he did, she bored him to extinction. Stimulating conversation was not her forte. She was monosyllabic. This, curiously enough, was part of her charm for many, who imagined that her thoughts, since seldom spoken, were deep. In a way they were. She was eaten alive by jealousy and anxiety. She was torn by agonies of impending disaster if her escort of the moment – Hugh was one in a line of young doctors who took her out for brief periods – paid too little attention to her. She tried not to show it, she struggled against the feelings themselves, but jealousy and rage possessed her again and again. Contrary to what Nicola and the secretaries at the Central imagined – they considered her silent, aloof, superior – she passed her time in a ferment. She was tortured by an impending conviction of unworthiness, which devastated her the moment she was unnoticed.

Unfortunately Hugh was inclined to neglect her. He was at this time extremely hard working, and in any case he looked on her more as an ornament to be displayed from time to time than as an intimate friend. He never came to know her well, partly because he made no effort to do so, but also because she deliberately set out to deceive him. She was, rightly, ashamed of her nature.

Hugh would soon have tired of her. The appearance of Nicola merely gave his parting from her an abruptness that it might otherwise have lacked. But the break was a shock to Angela, and she was not helped by her consciousness that Hugh had dropped her for the other girl. This was a blow to her pride, and confirmation of her worst fears. She seethed with a longing to get her own back – on Nicola, on Hugh, on the world. She held prolonged imaginary conversations with all her acquaintances, in which she disparaged Hugh Ravelston, while her hearers agreed. She prophesised, in these unspoken dialogues, a sticky end for Hugh Ravelston. He would go too far one day.

There seemed little likelihood of this, though. He obtained the Membership the first time he sat for it. He was Vanstone's registrar, which while no sinecure, was one of the most coveted posts. He was fully involved in off-shore racing, and for the first time, as a result of Rodney's departure for the Antarctic, helmed *Opening Snap*, the Sailing Club Pionier, and raced her to hard-won victory in the Dinard Race. This was a triumph that pleased him enormously. This and the Membership – he felt wonderful. There was nothing he could not achieve, once he set his mind to it.

He was in constant demand at parties, of course, as he had always been, though he seldom any longer stayed till dawn. He was in fact beginning to sober down, though few noticed this. He still looked in at the pub in the evening, with the rest of the crowd, but he had no time to stay there in one of the argumentative groups that would afterwards move off in a body to eat somewhere, perhaps see a show, and then go on to someone's flat for coffee and more talk until the small hours.

It was in the pub, though, that he first became conscious of Nicola. This was the end of the hard work and the early nights. She was there with a friend of his, and from that moment he could never understand how she could have been around the hospital for six months without his knowledge. How could he have failed to see her?

Angela was forgotten. There had never been a girl like Nicola before. Nicola with her grace and her fragile charm. Never again would he let her out of his sight.

She had not the slightest intention that he should.

He took her over from that evening. They left the pub together – she heartlessly left poor Ken standing, and he failed to collect Angela for the theatre – and went for a meal in Soho, where they gazed, entranced, across the white tablecloth at one another, and twirled the red wine in their glasses while they told each other their life's history.

From that night they were together. Nicola would go searching for Hugh in the wards, in outpatients – to the annoyance of numerous sisters and staff nurses – and when she found him she would sit waiting for him to be ready to leave. Then she would snuggle up against him in the car, and they would drive out to the country for a meal. Or sometimes they would drive purposelessly, merely for the joy of being together, uninterrupted, in their own tiny, enclosed little world. Hugh loved those evenings most of all, when they shared a spiritual and physical intimacy that he seemed to have lost since childhood. The comfort of Nicola's presence warmed him through to the marrow, and he would have been content to have driven for ever like this.

Not so Nicola. She liked to show him off. She was prepared to enjoy the quiet evenings when they were alone, because she was enraptured with Hugh, and to be with him was contentment. But what she liked most was to be seen about with him, to be taken by him into those Ravelston circles that she would never otherwise have entered. From Sailing Club dances to stuffy medical receptions, she went to them all at Hugh's side and savoured the triumph of being his chosen girl-friend – Hugh Ravelston's girl-friend, the very words had glamour, and the reality was almost more than she could bear, it was so satisfying. She was delighted, too, to succeed the beautiful – though admittedly weird – Angela Carlton. She had watched Angela from afar, and had considered her the height of sophisticated elegance. Nicola was too young, too thoughtless, and too wrapped up in Hugh himself, to imagine the possibility of the other girl's heartache – if it was indeed heartache, and not temper, which most of them at the Central thought more likely.

For Nicola, Hugh opened the door into so many new and spacious worlds. Her own existence, in her own eyes, glittered, so that even if she had not been in love with him, she would have been in a trance of delight. There was so much to do, to see, to join, and all the while there was Hugh as well, the perfect companion, the admired partner. Hugh, with his Alfa-Romeo. Angela had appreciated this, too. Hugh, the most brilliant of the young registrars at the Central, frowning over the case-papers in his hand, aloof, white-coated, his eyes lighting up as he caught sight of her. Hugh, sailing *Opening Snap*, driving her down to East Callant in the Alfa first, leaving her at the George with the wives and girl-friends, returning tired and relaxed from sun and wind, his hair tousled, his great sweater smelling of salt, his feet clumsy in sea boots, his arm securely round her, while they all argued unintelligibly over whether they could get more speed out of her if the Jenny were

26

cut lower. She adored the life she led with Hugh almost as much as she adored Hugh himself.

She met Rodney Ravelston, just before he went out to the Antarctic, and his wife Emma. Rodney took Nicola for a gentle sail in *Sea Goose*, his own boat. Nicola was exhilarated. This was the life. She and Hugh went to dinner with Rodney and Emma several times. Emma was dull, Nicola thought. Of course, she was pregnant, but surely that didn't mean that she need not bother at all about her appearance? She sat about in fearfully ordinary cotton smocks, her hair pushed back behind a band. She hardly joined the conversation, simply sat there with them knitting or else went off to the kitchen to prepare a meal. Nicola knew that she ought to have gone with her to help, but she preferred to stay with the men, where the conversation was lively, and she was the centre of attraction.

She met Sir Donald Ravelston once or twice. She found him frightening, he was so very grand and old, and totally unresponsive to her, which was disconcerting.

He had taken an instant dislike to her.

'Another Annabel,' he said accusingly to Rodney, as though Rodney were in some way responsible for Nicola's existence. 'She'll be no good to him, any more than Annabel was to poor Andrew. However, it's their affair. I couldn't stop Andrew marrying a fool, and I certainly shan't attempt to stop Hugh. There's hardly any Ravelston in him, in any case.' He did not know how to be more disparaging than this.

Nicola put him out of her mind. She had other men to think about. Above all, Hugh.

Now her flat, her lovingly-contrived Bohemian background, came into its own. Nicola's flat was scruffy and charming. Off the Finchley Road, it had been the kitchen of one of those great Edwardian houses gone to seed. It had its own entrance – the back door – which gave on to a long passage. At one end was what had been a pantry, and a door leading into a paved area, and at the other the kitchen itself. Nicola had painted the passage scarlet, and the pantry was her kitchen and bathroom. She had to go into the area to reach the lavatory, and she had a tub of geraniums growing by the door.

'The door with geraniums outside, darling. You must admit, it isn't everyone who has geraniums growing outside the loo.'

The old kitchen was vast – twenty by thirty feet, and with a great bay window overlooking the garden, flooded with the setting sun. There was the old kitchen range at the opposite end of the room, and Nicola had painted it wedgwood blue and white, and scattered it with a froth of glass animals, Christmas bells, stars, and coloured balls, candles, mobiles, pot plants. Her bed was a four-poster hung with muslin, which she kept drawn virginally. Or so she asserted.

This affair with Hugh was the real thing, she told everyone. She had always known that one day she would find a great love. Hugh was different from anyone else she had known.

She found him surprisingly reserved, though, she said to her girl-friends. He did not confide in her. Other men, whom she had loved less, had told her far more about themselves. She had learned more about them in a couple of weeks than she found out about Hugh in a year. Hugh was easy and sociable, she said, he gave no appearance of being remote, quite the opposite. But he shared only the surface of his life. His deeper feelings he kept to himself. Once or twice Nicola found herself on forbidden ground. She knew this by the way Hugh shied off, changed the conversation. Nicola had an instinct for noting a withdrawal in a relationship, however slight. It brought her up short, piqued her, challenged her.

Hugh, she came to realise, withdrew if any mention was made of his mother, Annabel. He seldom referred to her. Not that he avoided mentioning her name. But he pretended that she played no part in his life, and this was obviously untrue. Perhaps he believed it himself?

One evening Nicola thought she was going to find out. They were both in her kitchen. Nicola was making sauce Bolognese, one of her standard dishes. Hugh watched her cutting onion, putting it into sizzling fat, then cutting great bulging field mushrooms, adding them to the onion. Then into the pan went the minced beef, pink and fleshy. He watched Nicola turning it over with a wooden spoon, and as she turned it the colour changed. He was fascinated. Next she was chopping tomatoes on her board, then it was red and green peppers, with a clean tangy smell. Bay leaves out of a jar, pepper and salt, garlic, cinnamon – the most splendid smell came from the dark mess in the pan.

All at once he longed to have her cooking like this for him every night, her face flushed, hair hanging damply across her high brow. Her neat little hands, her bony fingers, whose touch he loved, now smelt pungently of food. She stepped delicately about her kitchen, and he knew he was at home there. He had not felt like this since he was a small boy, living with Annabel in the cottage at East Callant. Afterwards, there had been no kitchen companionship. The Ravelstons were a masculine society, in which Jean functioned more as a school matron than as the heart of a family.

'How cosy it can be in a kitchen,' he

exclaimed, remembering. 'When I was a little boy my mother and I–' he broke off.

'Your mother and you?' Nicola queried, looking up from the pan, the wooden spoon poised.

'Nothing,' he said vaguely. He found that he didn't, after all, feel like discussing it. 'Let's talk about you. Do you realise, Nicky, that for a thoroughly decorative and attractive piece of homework, you are quite extraordinarily talented?'

Of course she had been delighted. It was only later that she understood that he had fobbed her off again. Hugh himself would not have considered that there was any meaning to be attached to his evasion. Simply, he was more interested in Nicola than in himself as a small boy. He watched her with love and possessiveness, his darling Nicola. It was then that he decided to marry her. They would have a home of their own, the two of them. He would come back in the evening to find her in the kitchen, stirring something on the stove that smelt delicious, and her eyes would light up for him. He would hold her tiny fragility in his arms. She would be all his, his alone.

The day that was to end all his hopes began deceptively well. He had not been called out during the night, he had gone to the wards early, everything had run comparatively smoothly, even Vanstone, who was becoming very touchy, had been in a good mood and had made one or two of his acidly amusing little jokes. Hugh had had a clear half-hour for lunch, which was exceptional, the afternoon clinic had begun punctually, no one's case papers had vanished without trace, no one's X-rays had been mislaid, there had been few major interruptions, and the clinic startlingly enough, had ended as punctually as it had begun. There had been no last minute call from the wards, he had spoken to Neville, Vanstone's house physician, and they had gone together to look at the patient in the corner bed in coma.

'We shan't have the lab results until tomorrow morning,' Hugh had said. 'So I think I'll push off now. I'll be back soon after midnight, I expect. Well, better say by one or two to be on the safe side. But I'll be around by then, if you want me. Meanwhile keep an eye on his airway.' He wondered momentarily if it was quite fair to Neville to go out of reach – it was the Yacht Club dance down at East Callant. Then he remembered how disappointed Nicola would be if he told her they could not go, and decided Neville would have to manage. Do him good to stand on his own feet, for once. Time he lost this habit of ringing Hugh every time he was wondering if he should give someone a Soneryl tablet.

He went to his room to change, and had

left the hospital by six. At seven he had collected Nicola and they were driving flat out down the Cambridge Road.

The dance had delighted Nicola. She always particularly enjoyed these Yacht Club occasions, and tonight she flowered brilliantly. She looked beautiful and very touching, in the dress Hugh had bought for her, a straight silk tunic of Art Nouveau swirling flowers in blue and green. The dress had been ludicrously expensive. Hugh had taken one look at it, in the window of a little shop in South Molton Street, where he was trying to park, and had known at once that it was Nicola's dress. She had no expensive clothes, as she was permanently short of money, and he had taken her off to buy it in the lunch hour the following day. Now she was wearing it, her hair, tonight, hanging loose and straight, her eyes huge and green. She was a feather in his arms as they danced, and her frailty drew the heart out of him. He held her tenderly, and thought that when they were alone, driving back to London, he would talk to her about their future and their marriage. She would like a ring, and perhaps tomorrow they would go out and buy one. An emerald, to match her eyes?

After the dance, they were to go on board *Moon Maid* for coffee before the drive back. Everyone was in a good humour, even the old man. On shore there were shouts and jokes, as people packed into their cars. They stood about on the jetty, the water rippled and gurgled at their feet, and the trees whispered above. They were deciding to sleep on board *Moon Maid,* have an early breakfast, and drive back – to London or Cambridge – the next morning. Nicola's eyes shone. She could think of nothing more romantic.

Hugh hated to disappoint her. 'Sorry,' he said. 'Count me out.'

'Oh, but *Hugh,*' half a dozen voices protested. 'Why on earth not? Plenty of time – start at six-thirty if you like.'

'Sorry,' he repeated. 'Nothing doing.'

'But surely–'

'Leave the boy alone,' his grandfather intervened. 'If he can't, he can't. He knows what his commitments are.'

'I told Neville he'd be able to get me tonight,' he said. 'We've got a chap in coma we haven't quite sorted out.'

'Better be off, then,' his grandfather said, briefly. 'It's midnight.'

'Stay, if you like, Nicola,' Jean said. She had seen the girl's evident disappointment. 'Don would drive you up in plenty of time in the morning – wouldn't you, Don?' Eager then to please a crestfallen child, it failed to occur to Jean that Hugh might not be entirely delighted to have his girl friend handed over to Don – who of course fielded her neatly.

'Pleasure,' he assured her immediately.

Don had not himself brought a girl down to the dance. There had been no one he cared for enough to make it worthwhile to pay for a ticket. Don had always had a pronounced streak of meanness.

'Oh, would you really?' Nicola breathed. 'Are you sure it would be all right?'

'Perfectly all right,' Jean said. 'We'd love to have you.'

'Absolutely all right. Company for me,' Don echoed. He could see that Hugh was annoyed, which always cheered him.

'How terribly kind of you. I should simply love to stay,' Nicola said. 'You don't mind, do you Hugh? I would adore to stay on.'

'Do exactly as you like,' he said. He was furious. He turned the car and drove back alone, seething, slamming the gears. There was gratitude for you. He bought the wretched girl her dress, paid for the tickets for this hideously expensive dance, and then the damned creature left him to drive back to London alone. What an ending to the evening. He shouldn't, he realised also, have had that last whisky. He must drive cautiously. He did drive cautiously, or what seemed to him at the time to be cautiously. In the years that followed he was constantly to ask himself whether if he had been stone-cold sober the driver of the other car might have escaped death. There was no answer to that. There never would be.

When the car came roaring across the road and slap into him, he wrenched the wheel round to try to evade the inevitable. Afterwards, he thought that if he had been at his best he would have accelerated and gone straight ahead, and he might have just missed the Ford. But to do that his mind would have had to have been working with clockwork precision. The fault was his, the other driver had the right of way, and Hugh had been driving too fast. He was in a built-up area, within a 40 m.p.h. limit. At that time of the night there was little on the road, and he had been doing sixty. He regarded this as cautious. He could have done eighty with impunity. Better if he had done, he often thought afterwards. He would have whistled by while the man in the Ford was still a quarter of a mile away. But he had been speeding, he had not had the right of way, and he had alcohol on his breath. He had not denied either the speed or the alcohol. The seriousness of the occasion, he felt, demanded the truth, and nothing else. No evasions, or half-truths.

This turned out to be a mistake. His future might have been entirely different if he had said nothing, or had told a downright lie. But he had been shocked and confused, his worldly knowledge was totally scattered, and he had come out with the damning truth.

This went against him in court. In due course they brought in a verdict of manslaughter, and took away his licence. The case made unpleasant headlines. The press appeared to dislike him on several different counts – he had been to Garside, to Cambridge, he was a doctor, his family had money and prestige and in addition a title. Not an inherited title, true, but his grandfather had a handle to his name, a house in Harley Street and another at East Callant, and a yacht, his mother lived on the continent with her second husband, his uncle was a don at Cambridge and as well known as his grandfather, one of his cousins also owned a yacht. Rolling in money, status and underserved possessions, the Ravelstons, and they had produced a play-boy and given him a lethal weapon, the Alfa-Romeo. All this was a useful example of the undesirability of wealth and privilege, especially among medical men, whom a number of journalists particularly disliked. Friends explained this to Hugh, but the headlines and insinuations written between the lines of the already stinging paragraphs burnt into him with some of the acid truth.

There were many at the Central who had always resented the easy path of the spoilt Ravelstons, with their grandeur and their cutting ironical tongues, coupled with their infuriating brilliance. They were not sorry to see one brought to book. Hugh especially had been too successful too soon and too easily, and some of his contemporaries were glad to see him crash down from the high place they considered he had unfairly inherited.

There were others who lacked envy, but who looked at him dispassionately, and considered he had reaped his just reward. They did not go out of their way to damn him. They thought he had damned himself. He read their cold judgement in their eyes, and had to admit it to be reasonable.

This was how Vanstone looked at it. Vanstone had no time now for his registrar. He would see, gossip said, that Hugh never had another post at the Central, Ravelston or not. Meanwhile Hugh had no sympathy from him, rather a cold and cutting impatience.

Vanstone, as luck would have it, had rung his registrar soon after midnight on the night of the accident. He had been put through instead to his house physician. This had infuriated him. His staff should be there when he needed them.

'Where's Ravelston?' he demanded.

'He's out, sir,' the terrified Neville had gabbled. 'He'll be back any minute now, I expect.'

'H'm. How's that patient in coma?'

'Well, sir, I'm – I'm not very happy about him.'

That did it. Vanstone felt savage. Ravelston had no right to be out, leaving that young half-wit on his own. He should be there on the ward. He began cross-examining Neville. 'C.S.F.? Pulse? Blood pressure?' None of the answers assuaged his irritation. Finally he snapped, 'Tell Ravelston to ring me here immediately he's had another look at the patient.'

Neville had rung Hugh, at ten-minute intervals, almost, from then onwards. At five o'clock, in desperation, he rang Vanstone. He had no alternative.

Vanstone, roused from sleep to find himself still talking to Neville had been rigid with fury. He took this out on Neville.

'Why didn't you let me know earlier?' What had been happening while he slept? He demolished his house physician, and announced that he would come straight round to the ward. He was in fact acutely worried. He had been comfortably asleep, imagining that Ravelston – up till now reliable – had been looking after the case. What was he going to find?

He examined the patient, terrorising Neville throughout the proceedings and bullying him unmercifully, and was writing the treatment in the case notes, when Hugh appeared. He did not present an edifying spectacle – unshaven, exhausted, worried, still wearing his dinner jacket, his shirt crumpled, his tie awry. Vanstone looked at him with icy dislike. 'Where have you been?'

Hugh apologised, and added that he had had an accident driving up from East Callant.

Vanstone raised his brows. 'You had been, I gather, to the – um – *Yacht* Club – um – function?' he enquired, pronouncing yacht club as though it had been thieves kitchen. Vanstone had no time for the sailing types at the Central. Philistine hearties, heavy drinking and bone-headed, he considered them all. He could hardly describe Sir Donald Ravelston or his sons and grandsons as bone from the neck up, the opposite was plainly apparent, but this annoyed him even more. To affect this degrading athletic pastime was unsuitable and irresponsible of them.

He looked Hugh up and down. 'An extraordinarily debauched appearance to present on the ward,' he remarked waspishly. 'In view of the fact that we have managed to get along tolerably well without you so far, I think you had better leave us. Go to your room and find some more suitable garments. Make some attempt to remedy your appearance. Difficult though it may be. We have a day's work ahead. Presumably you are – er – prepared to – um – share our labours? You are quite sure you have no other social engagements of a pressing nature?'

Hugh mumbled and apologised again. But it made no difference. As far as Vanstone was concerned, he was finished. From then on, Vanstone gave him no quarter. Hugh could not blame him. He knew he had brought this on himself. At the Central doctors were not meant to have any private life until they reached consultant status. Vanstone was conscientious himself, and to him Hugh's behaviour was outrageous.

It was outrageous to others besides Vanstone. Now Hugh found out what it was like not to be the blue-eyed boy. Now he was the unreliable Ravelston, on whom they could none of them depend. He was, also, the Ravelston who had let them down, who had made the Central the focus of undesirable publicity. He had let down the hospital and his profession, and they had no scruples in telling him so. They all knew he was finished. At teaching hospitals like the Central there was no room for a mistake.

Everyone, he knew, was looking askance at him. Not merely his seniors. Sisters, students, radiographers, physiotherapists, even the ward maids and porters. Some of them were heavily disapproving, others watching him only because he was in the news. He felt all the glances as arrows of judgement.

III

Hugh went down to East Callant. He had to go and face his grandfather.

Although the Ravelstons still had the house in Harley Street – divided now into consulting-rooms and flats, and making them an excellent income – where Sir Donald Ravelston had lived and practised for half a century, he lived now for most of the year in Harbour Cottage, looking out across the estuary.

This had been Hugh's childhood home, but Annabel and all her charming clutter were gone. The cottage held nothing, now, of her gaiety. Instead the rooms were filled with the old man's tall bookcases, the windows were curtained with Jean's practical choice of bottle-green velvet. There was a smell of cigars, whisky and tar, no longer of hyacinths and *Nuit de Longchamps,* and the atmosphere was far from welcoming.

The old man was at his most formidable. Hugh found it difficult to face him, so much controlled displeasure emanated from his gaunt frame. He received his youngest grandson seated at his large desk, an attitude often adopted in former years when interviewing recalcitrant students, and one which came naturally to him.

'Well?' he demanded.

He knew the outline, of course. Hugh had written to him, and Archie had telephoned as a result, had catechised him, and had, he knew, passed all the answers on to his father. Both of them, in addition, had almost certainly discussed the affair with others at the Central – Archie, Hugh had reason to suspect, with Michael Vanstone, which would not have helped him. His grandfather had been to see Professor Ramsay, his successor. This knowledge was not calculated to make Hugh feel any more at his ease.

'I'm sorry about this,' he said. It seemed the least he could say, and, God knew, it was the truth.

'Why did you allow it to happen?'

'Well, I – er – I–' What was he supposed to answer to that? He hadn't allowed it to happen. If there had been any question of allowing it, he would not be in this position, blast it. 'I don't think – I – I don't see how I could have – it wasn't–' His grandfather always succeeded in having this effect on him. He was at his worst when confronted with him.

'Don't make excuses.'

Hugh was still standing before the wide desk, like a small boy up for judgement. He shuffled his feet, as he would have done in boyhood days. Matters, however, were a good deal worse now than they could ever have been then.

'What were you thinking of to leave the Central when you had this patient in coma?'

'Well, I – I should have been back in time to see how he was going on. I should have–'

'Don't tell me what you *should* have been. *Were* you back in time?'

'No.'

'Exactly. Then perhaps you'll give me an answer to my question.'

'I thought I'd be back in time.' He knew this answer would damn him.

'You thought.' The old man paused nastily. 'Did you take any steps to ensure that you were?'

'I suppose not.'

'You left here at midnight. In my opinion, of course, you should never have been away from the Central at all. But I'm trying to be fair.'

Like hell you are, Hugh thought bitterly.

'Assuming – which I personally can't accept – assuming, however, that you were justified in leaving the Central, what possible excuse had you for remaining here until midnight?'

'None, I suppose. But it didn't occur to me at the time that–'

'It didn't occur to you. Very likely not.' He allowed another unpleasant silence to fall, and then added, 'But if you had even the rudiments of a sense of responsibility it would have occurred to you.'

The conversation continued, covering in detail the question of whether Hugh should have left London that evening, why he had found it necessary to attend the Yacht Club dance at all, why, if he had done so, he had failed to leave early, why he had had anything to drink when he knew he would be driving back, why he had driven to London too fast, and why he had been speeding in a restricted area.

'Everybody does it,' Hugh muttered feebly.

'Everybody? Everybody? And since when have the Ravelstons been everybody?'

There was no answer to this one.

His grandfather regarded him in silence, and Hugh dropped his eyes to the carpet, though he tried not to. Finally came the last accusatory question.

'How can you call yourself a doctor when you have less sense of responsibility for the lives of other human beings than the average layman? How do you expect people to trust themselves, or their families, their wife or child, to your care? Eh?' The old man sighed. He was genuinely shocked and depressed, though Hugh failed to notice this and saw only the anger and displeasure. 'Careless on the roads. Careless in the wards.'

This stung. Hugh thought it unfair, but he knew better, by now, than to protest.

'Apparently it was nothing to you that you had a dying patient in your care. You had a dance to go to.'

Hugh mumbled uncomfortably. It had not been like that at all.

'You might conceivably have weighed this up before you set out – and again before you drank so much. I trust that the General Medical Council will find themselves able to take a more lenient view than I can.'

The General Medical Council?

'You look startled,' his grandfather said. 'Had it not occurred to you that if you are found guilty in a court of law – which seems to me likely in the circumstances, though admittedly I am not familiar with these proceedings – the verdict will be reported to the General Medical Council?'

Hugh found his mouth had dried.

'You can rely on me to see that you have the best legal advice,' the old man added, briskly. 'I have already made enquiries, and Blennerhasset will be in touch with you.'

Hugh muttered apologetic thanks.

'Not at all,' his grandfather responded unkindly. 'Unfortunately you are my grandson, and you bear the Ravelston name.' The glance accompanying this statement was unmistakable, and cut Hugh deeply. He tried to hide its pain by telling himself that his grandfather had finally become senile. He was behaving like someone out of an Edwardian novelette. 'You are a disgrace to our fair name. Leave this house, sir, and never darken my towels again,' as they had once cried in ringing tones in the course of a parody they had put on one term in the house at Garside.

This diversion, though, failed to work. The clear rejection remained with him, burnt into him. Especially the final words, spoken, at last, not in anger but reflectively, almost to himself, an old man's forgetfulness of the presence of others. 'I never thought you'd make a doctor. It isn't in you. You're Annabel's boy.' Old Donald Ravelston was regretting his lost son Andrew, always his favourite, and remembering, too, his mistaken marriage.

'I saw from the beginning she would be nothing but a liability,' he told Archie. 'Now look what she has made of that boy. Thank heavens you had the foresight to marry someone sensible. Jean's always been a tower of strength.'

Archie was amused, and repeated this to Jean.

'Indeed?' she said. 'I'm delighted to hear it. I'd be even more delighted if either of you two opinionated men showed the least sign of being a tower of strength to poor Hugh, in all his difficulties.'

'Eh?' Archie gaped at her. She seldom turned on him like this, and he didn't understand what she was driving at.

'That poor boy. And all the old man can do is blame Annabel. Why doesn't he blame himself? Oh, you Ravelstons, what a tiresome lot you are.'

'I think all this is most uncalled for,' Archie said sniffily. 'We've always done everything possible for Hugh.'

Jean sighed irritably. 'Oh, I know, I know. We've provided a roof over his head, and I've always sent him back to Garside with his socks mended and the right number of shirts.'

'We're all very fond of him,' Archie pointed out coldly.

'Rodney's the only one who's ever done anything that mattered about Hugh. And where's Rodney now, just when he's needed? Stuck in a hut somewhere near the South Pole. I ask you?'

'Really, Jean, you're being quite unreasonable.'

'Reason won't help Hugh.'

Archie sighed. 'I must say, I find it very difficult to be at all sympathetic. Why on earth the young fool–'

'I know you don't feel sympathetic. No one does. That's the trouble.'

'There's Annabel,' Archie suggested dubiously.

Jean snorted. 'Annabel loves Annabel.'

'I'm afraid you're right. Well, what is it you want me to do?'

'I don't know. I wish I did. Try and stop the old man giving Hugh such hell, perhaps.'

Archie spoke to his father, but he found himself speaking to deaf ears. Donald Ravelston wanted to hear nothing further about his youngest grandson. 'Blennerhasset will be dealing with it. I've done all I can. I don't want to hear any more about him. Thoroughly irresponsible. Can't be trusted to look after a hamster, let alone a sick human being. Would you be inclined to trust Jean to his care, eh?'

This sort of talk soon began to spread through the Central. Hugh's own friends were worried, but they were unable to stop the malicious gossip. He'd simply have to live it down, they told one another. Of course, he had an ordeal before him yet, when his case came before the Disciplinary Committee of the G.M.C. This would be a highly unpleasant formality. At the worst, though, he would be reprimanded.

Here they were wrong. They were so sure he would escape – after all, he was Sir Donald Ravelston's grandson. This, in fact, may have gone against him. Justice must not only be done, but be seen to be done. What was medicine coming to? And on top of everything else, there was this unsavoury story about some girl who was a patient. This sort of behaviour could not be tolerated.

The Disciplinary Committee was not

prepared to tolerate it. A young man might have been given the benefit of the doubt as far as his driving was concerned, but never when it came to any question of an illicit relationship with a patient. Here there was no room for understanding or pity. Members of the Committee were agreed that they could not allow their sympathies to sway them in this context. Hugh's position was hopeless.

The patient in question was Angela Carlton. She had written to one of the members whom she knew as a consultant at the Central, alleging that Hugh had had an affair with her after he first met her as a patient. She gave details of her attendance at the clinic.

At the Central, of course, they all knew that Hugh Ravelston had had an affair with Angela Carlton. He denied that he had ever treated her as a patient. The consultant who had received the letter discussed the matter with Michael Vanstone, who by this time was ready to believe anything of his registrar. When it came to a decision, the Committee found itself in doubt about Hugh's truthfulness. It was already, naturally, in a considerably greater doubt about Angela Carlton's truthfulness, but it was Hugh Ravelston's professional integrity that was up for judgement.

Hugh Ravelston was off the medical register.

Stunned, he had returned to the Central. He thought he had been living in a nightmare for months, but this was unspeakably worse. Vanstone had been coldly correct. There was nothing to be done but to hand over his cases – to Ben, of all people, who had been going on ten days' holiday. He had even done poor old Ben out of his deserved holiday. What a shambles.

Only the necessity to write up his case notes meticulously and to hand them over to Ben kept the nightmare temporarily at bay. The work – done against time – and the concentration required interposed a curtain between him and reality, between him and the interested glances that followed him. Many of them thought he cared little.

The day after the news broke, Professor Ramsay, who had succeeded his grandfather as Professor of Medicine, had sent for him.

'There's a story going round about a girl who was a patient here – is there anything in it?'

'Angela Carlton, sir. I had an affair with her.'

'Had she been a patient?'

'Not to my knowledge. I'm sure I never treated her, sir. I couldn't have forgotten. She has been a patient here, though.'

'I see.' Ramsay sighed. Did he believe Ravelston? Difficult to say. He sighed again. 'I – I'm sorry, Ravelston. This is an appalling affair.' He leaned back in his chair and began lighting his pipe. Then he looked up. 'I'd like you to tell me, quite off the record. No action to be taken either way. Are you sure she was never a patient of yours?'

'If she was I've forgotten. I can't believe she was.'

'Are you being evasive?'

It hadn't occurred to Hugh that his answer might have sounded like an attempt to avoid an outright lie.

'No,' he said. 'To my knowledge I've never treated her, sir. I think she's made it all up.'

'Why?'

'I'm afraid I rather dropped her.'

'A woman scorned, eh?'

'I suppose so.' Angela was weird, of course. But he still found it almost impossible to believe that she had gone as far as this. He looked, at that moment, very young, and incredulous, and Ramsay decided to believe him.

'All right,' he said abruptly. 'What are you going to do now?'

Hugh didn't know.

'Are you all right for money?' First things first, Alec Ramsay always insisted.

'Yes, thank you, sir.'

Ramsay thought this likely. After all, he knew the Ravelstons.

'Then why not take a holiday of some sort? You've had a wearing time. Go sailing, eh? Something like that? Put a bit of time between you and this nasty shock.'

'No,' Hugh was astonished to hear himself saying. 'No, I must work. I must find a job at once.'

Ramsay gave him a keen glance. He was surprised. Then, to Hugh's utter amazement, he said, 'All right, m'boy. I daresay I can find you one somewhere.'

These were the first kind words Hugh had had from any of his seniors, and he nearly broke down. He flushed, swallowed, and said in sardonic tones exactly like those of his cousin Don, 'In a zoo, perhaps?' Then horror-struck, he realised that he had been insufferably rude.

But Ramsay took no notice. He simply went on, in calm unaltered tones, 'I'll find you something to do for the next few weeks, and then we'll have a chance to see how the land lies.' He gave Hugh a long considering look, which Hugh interpreted as a summing up of his entire failed career, but which in fact had merely been an assessment that he was still in a state of shock, and that it would be useless to embark on any detailed discussion about the future. 'Come back tomorrow,' he said, opening his book, 'and we'll have another little chat, eh? At four-thirty,' he added, writing it down.

'Thank you, sir,' Hugh said, in a defeated voice that no one else at the Central was to hear from him. He let himself out into the corridor. He found he was shaking.

He also found Ben propping up the wall, waiting for him. He was unable to meet his eyes, he again felt the impending collapse of all his defences. He grabbed at Ben's arm as he went blindly by. The gesture was intended as a friendly signal of recognition in passing, but to Ben it felt like the clutch of desperation. Hugh found that Ben was apparently glued to his side, and that suddenly he was in Ben's old Morris 1000. There, in the tiny car, he did finally break down. There was only Ben to see, thank God. He made some mumbled apology, shuddering and snorting, and blowing his nose.

'A good thing too,' Ben said unexpectedly. 'I was getting a bit tired of this stiff upper lip stuff. Phony as hell.'

Ben and Hugh had been together since they were newly-arrived thirteen-year-olds at Garside, Hugh thin and nervy, Ben square and solid. They made a useful team. Yet even with Ben, Hugh had remained basically reserved, had tried to hide pain or defeat – usually unsuccessfully, but this of course was unknown to him. Now it was so no longer. With Ben the barriers were down for all time – yet neither of them was ever to mention this episode.

At the Central they did mention it, at considerable length. In fact, it was well chewed over. The grapevine had done its work, and the entire medical staff was apparently aware that H.D. Ravelston had seen Professor Ramsay, had come out looking like death and had been hustled away, looking as if he would crumple at any minute, by Ben Calderwood.

'Ramsay must have given him hell,' they announced with relish.

'After all,' someone pointed out, 'it can't be often that Ramsay has a chance to demolish a Ravelston. The boot, one suspects, has been frequently on the other foot.' Ramsay had been Sir Donald Ravelston's registrar, many years back. 'One can't blame him for making the most of the unexpected opportunity.'

In fact Donald Ravelston and Ramsay had had an argument about Hugh.

'I think you're being too hard on the boy,' Ramsay had said.

'H'mph.'

'I know he was at fault in the first instance, but I don't believe this story about the girl – and in any case the poor fellow has undoubtedly reaped the whirlwind.'

'Asked for it. In my day–' Sir Donald Ravelston related an anecdote, well known to all at the Central, about Sir James Manningham Lawther, who had expected his houseman to remain within the hospital for the entire six months of his appointment.

When an otherwise satisfactory young man had had the temerity once to be missing for two hours – after four months service – Lawther had told him to pack his bags at once. That had been the end of any chance of a career at his teaching hospital.

'Out of date,' Ramsay said shortly.

'Daresay. But a sense of responsibility will never be out of date in medicine.'

'He's not as irresponsible as you think. I like the boy.'

'Glad someone does. Damned young fool.'

'It's a great pity this has happened,' Ramsay said firmly. 'I had formed great hopes of him. If I may say so, he has far more of you in him than any of the others of your family, and I looked forward to seeing him grow in stature, and eventually do this hospital great credit.'

'H'mph. Well, you were wrong, weren't you, eh?' The old man stalked off. But he was pleased, though he wouldn't admit it. Perhaps there was good stuff in the boy after all. Had he been too hard on him? Then he thought the affair over, and decided he had been right in the first instance. Damn it, there wasn't only the fast driving, the neglect of his patient, the drinking. That was bad enough. But there was also the girl. Or rather, the two girls. The one he had dropped in order to run after that chit Nicola something-or-other. But before he had dropped the first girl he had managed not only to make love to her, but to have her as a patient. Outrageous. Conscienceless. Disreputable. Ramsay was mistaken in him. He had always been too easy-going, disposed to be sentimental about patients and colleagues alike.

Ramsay had something of the same thoughts himself. He was being a fool over the Ravelston boy. In his compassion for the poor fellow, with his career ruined, he had gone too far.

However, he decided typically, what did it matter? Hardly anyone had a kind word to spare for the boy. There was room for a little understanding and kindness. No need to add to the chorus of recrimination. The poor fellow had to take his punishment, that was out of his hands. He was finished as far as medicine was concerned. All that was left to do was to temper the wind. 'Let us have a little Christian charity occasionally, in this institution said to be for the care of the sick and suffering,' he announced to his colleagues.

When Hugh presented himself next day he found that Ramsay had unearthed an occupation for him. In the Medical School library there were cardboard cartons, thick with dust, filled with letters, case notes, jottings, all belonging to a physician who had died, ten years earlier. He had left his books and papers to the Medical School. The books had long ago been catalogued, but there had never been time to attack the papers. Ramsay now had them moved to his own consulting-rooms, where they annoyed his secretary intensely.

'You can have a month,' he said to Hugh. 'Do whatever you can in that time. Some sort of sorting into sections, and at least a pre-liminary cataloguing. No one knows what's there – private letters, practice letters, cor-respondence with journals, drafts for papers – some of them published, some not – case notes, plans, committee papers. I don't want to find it a muddle half done. You've got to achieve some sort of order and system.'

For a month he went there daily, and succeeded in producing order from chaos. The weeks passed. He was unable to shake himself out of a state of disbelief. He passed the time as if he were once again a student doing an odd job during his vacation. Soon this interim period would end. This he knew. But he was unable to comprehend that it would finish in anything other than a resumption of his usual activities. He tried to bring the truth home to himself, and knew a lurch of fear on each occasion. But the time passed, and he failed to comprehend.

Ramsay asked him if he had any plans. He had none, except this unalterable determin-ation to find a job, a routine job he knew it would have to be, within the medical world. He was possessed by this, his only objective.

58

He almost felt as though he was running away from some unknown alternative.

After a couple of weeks Ramsay told him that Dr Calderwood wanted a research assistant down at Brookhampton. He was the group pathologist there, and needed some work done to complete a small research project.

This was Ben's father. He was being looked after, Hugh realised. He had never before been in need of this sort of help, and he knew he should be grateful. Instead he was ashamed of his need, almost hostile. But he could not afford to do anything but accept, and not only accept, but show the gratitude he was unable to feel. What sort of post could he find without the personal intervention of some kindly senior colleague?

Colleague? Medical men, senior or junior, were no longer his colleagues, he reminded himself bitterly. He no longer belonged to their world.

He travelled down to Brookhampton for the interview. Since his boyhood, when he had occasionally stayed with Ben's family, he had met Jock Calderwood only briefly, at college occasions, rugger matches, hospital dances. In appearance, Jock Calderwood was Ben – thirty years on. The same sturdy figure, square jaw and piercing, almost black eyes. Ben's were set under ferocious black brows and a mass of unruly dark hair.

His father had a mop of grey hair, and jutting white eyebrows. Now he was to be his chief – if he were lucky. Hugh did not know how to handle the new relationship, and began on terms of the utmost formality.

A week later he was working in Brookhampton.

The full realisation hit him. This was to be his existence. Until now, he had been living in the moment, grimly determined to weather the storm, to make some sort of life for himself. This was it, and he was cut off from all he had taken for granted. His career was shattered. There was no next step. This was not an interim post to bridge a gap. This was his new job, and the days would go by like this indefinitely. Magnificently unprepared, he thought sardonically, for the long littleness of life. Except that there was nothing magnificent about it.

Again he faced it, still with astonishment. The past was irrevocable. He had left the Central for ever.

He sank into lethargy. There was nothing, it seemed, but routine and regret, and Brookhampton. He was not at his best. He could not even serve Jock Calderwood as usefully as the average technician, he found. He, the brilliant Hugh Ravelston. He was less proficient than a technician, and he was unable to control his thoughts, so that day after day he wasted time.

Not only was he a failure as a doctor, but he was not much use as a laboratory worker. What sort of an individual was he?

For years he had been reasonably confident. He had been popular, he had been in demand, he had felt sure of his own capabilities. Now this was all gone, he was deprived of the privileges that he had thoughtlessly accepted, and he could not even justifiably assume that he was better than average. He could see for himself that he was not.

Most of all, just now, he longed for companionship. Yet he evaded it when it was offered.

He was not ready for it. He was not ready to come out of himself. He was absent-minded, lost in his thoughts, his regrets, disliked being disturbed. He had lived in the midst of friends and colleagues always, perpetually on the move from one project to another, accompanied by a crowd of friendly faces. Now he chose to be alone, and spent his time dreaming. For the thoughts and memories came flocking in, whenever he raised his head from the microscope, they flooded in and he drowned himself in them. He was no fit company for anyone, and at lunch or coffee he often failed to hear what they said to him, so that they considered him aloof and superior – the fatal Ravelston nose with its hauteur added to the impression they already had in the pathology laboratory that he considered them all beneath his notice.

There was so much to think over, to try to face. Then too, there was the added difficulty that he did not know how to talk about himself, how much to tell them, when would be the right moment – if any could be – to explain about his past. So that conversation, when it did come, was subject to abrupt halts, embarrassed pauses, strange silences. He knew he was skating on thin ice. It was not exactly that he was ashamed of his own story. Or at least, let's face it, he argued with himself, I am ashamed of it and so I should be. But the silences came because suddenly into the phrases of a trivial conversation at lunch he could not consider flinging his dramatic history, announcing 'I was a medical registrar at the Central London Hospital until I was struck off.' This would only embarrass them, shouted across the table, and ruin their digestions, or his own, at any rate. This was something that could be confided, but not yelled. So when they asked 'Where were you before?' he merely replied curtly 'in London.' When they persevered, and asked 'what hospital?' he answered briefly and asked some question about a test, or the pudding, to change the subject. They were not fools, they soon knew he had something to hide. However, if he had no wish to tell it, they had no intention of dragging it out of him. Let him keep himself to himself, if that was what he wanted. They had offered friendship, he had rebuffed them. They left him alone, and seldom expected him to join them.

He was in a false position, had been from the beginning. They often criticised the doctors on the staff. They were a freemasonry that excluded medical men, whom they half resented, half envied, and whose knowledge of laboratory techniques they mocked. 'Little tin gods' they called them, and he felt constantly that he should have made it clear from the beginning that he had once been among them. Now it was too late, he had led his present colleagues, inadvertently, into expressing themselves in a way they would not have done if they had known his story. Or at least, they would have done it deliberately, challenging him, aware of his own interest. He knew he had been sly and deceitful, yet at first he had thought it not only easy but reasonable, sensible, to start afresh, with a clean slate, nothing from the past, nothing for them to know of lost triumphs, lost success. He would be just another technician, from anywhere, come to join them, with no pretensions to former status or regrets for a career blasted. No bid for sympathy, no attempt to hold the centre of the stage. But he found, of course, that every world is peopled by individuals with a past and a future, with goals to be worked for, families and girl friends and remembered loyalties. By disowning all this he made himself the centre of speculation, a strange misfit. They assumed he had disgraced himself, wondered if he could have served a prison sentence.

He saw he had begun wrongly with them. He had no energy now to alter matters. He was preoccupied and tired with the mere struggle to keep going, to put one foot down in front of the other, to rise and shave and have breakfast and reach the hospital at the right time, to work solidly through the repetitive chores, to keep his recollections at bay and to concentrate on good accurate work, again and again, and yet again. Not to stare out of the window, letting pain and futile recollections sweep through him and devour the working day.

Life at the Central had been very different. Every minute packed. Never time enough for all he wanted to crowd in. In fact, he had been overdoing it, crowding too much in. He had slipped into a way of life in which he expected to wake feeling as though he had been slugged, dependent on strong black coffee to revive him. He was tired. From the moment he unwillingly rose, there was no stop until, too late, he fell into bed for another few hours' sleep.

Every day saw the same pace. First the

wards, then too late to lunch, arguments and interruptions over the meal, with telephone calls from the wards, and then a quick dash to outpatients. When the last patient had been seen, and Vanstone had taken himself off, leaving a sheaf of instructions, there were letters to be dictated, back to the wards, a snatched cup of tea somewhere or other, telephone calls to the labs, to the X-ray department, to outside doctors. If nothing unusual happened – and when didn't it? More sensible to call it usual – when the usual failed to happen, and there was no emergency admission, no unexpected reaction, no one dying, no one suddenly putting up a fight for life, no lecture, demonstration or conference, then he might leave about seven, to have a meal with Nicola. She had probably been hanging around since six, waiting more and more impatiently, so that sometimes he cut the lecture, or the last discussion with Vanstone's house physician.

He and Nicola would go across the road to the pub, and he would have a whisky to ease the tension that had always built up by that hour, then they would have supper. Sometimes they went to her flat, and she cooked. More often they went out together, or made up a party. They would usually end at Nicola's flat in the small hours, and then, too exhausted to make love to her as he had hoped to do, he drove back to the hospital.

A last look in at the wards, and then bed.

When he had a week-end free it was booked up for months ahead, for sailing, rugger or some long-promised visit. This was all hard going, but fun, and he prided himself on working hard and playing hard, never defaulting on any of his commitments. He asserted that he enjoyed the pace. Yet on first waking he would have given anything to be able to turn over and go to sleep all morning. It was a crowded existence, filled with striving, stimulus, worry, achievement, narrow escapes and small triumphs. He had imagined no other. Not for him the dreams others had, of desert islands, single-handed cruises to the Caribbean, or remote crofts on the west coast of Scotland. He liked his life, where one evening he could meet Nicola in the pub with a crowd, go out with her to a show, wake to a full day at the hospital, then the following evening be driving out of London, to have supper on board *Opening Snap*, with the prospect of a hard sail ahead. This had been the life for him, he had always told them.

Now, at Brookhamton, he was tempted, often, to take the easy way out, to abandon this treadmill, to pack it all in and go to join Annabel in Switzerland. Why not forget the past in sun and long lazy days? Why not climb all day and drink in hilarious company all evening? Why struggle? He could have a long holiday, and then Simon or Annabel would soon find him something interesting to do. There he would be no failed doctor without a future. He would be Annabel's eldest son, part of her gay and glittering world, in which he could play a part – he could, for instance, have an executive post in some film or theatre company, learn how to run a picture gallery or an antique shop, write scripts, teach biology, chemistry, at one of the moneyed schools there, with ample time for ski-ing, skating, climbing. He could join Annabel's cosmopolitan existence, living in the flat in winter and the mountain chalet in summer. In short, he could join a circle where once again all doors would be opened for him, as they had once been at the Central.

This pleasant alternative was his unceasing conflict. When he was not lost in regret for his days at the Central, he was arguing with himself as to whether he should leave Brookhampton.

Why not? How in the name of sanity could he prefer Brookhampton and what amounted to a technician's job, and the dull tedium of weary days on the fringe of medicine? He chose it because try as he might, he was unable to leave medicine. Medicine might leave him, he thought bitterly, but he still stuck around. He was willing, when it came to it, to pay any price to remain. Medicine held him despite himself, meant something to him that he could not express or understand, but that at some fundamental level he refused to relinquish. Partly, of course, it was the old story. He wanted to prove himself a true Ravelston, despite appearances to the contrary. Then, too, there was a side to his personality that had no wish to follow the easy road, that desired struggle and difficulty, that understood growth came only through effort. Ultimately, there was his grandfather's rejection. He'd show the old devil.

Small wonder that in the midst of this battle with himself he had no energy to remake his relationships with his new colleagues.

He longed for the deliverance of Nicola's love. But he had to do without this, too. They had not been so close after his crash. They had continued to go out together, but he had been worried, distant, distracted, and he had not liked to make demands on her, while longing, always, for her to show him all the understanding he needed.

Now he was down in Brookhampton he hardly saw her. He had never supposed that he would miss her so acutely, that he would have to endure this actual physical ache of desire for her. In addition to his loneliness and despondency, the intolerable boredom of the routine work he was beginning to hate, there was this anguished longing for the comfort of her warm flesh. He wanted her to cherish him, to restore him, to demonstrate to him that his life still had meaning. Finally he asked her down to Brookhampton one Sunday.

It was not a success. He was living in lodgings in Malden Road, found by Mrs Calderwood. He didn't, at that time, care much where he stayed, and it seemed sensible to follow Mrs Calderwood's suggestion. Then, when he first met her, he was favourably impressed by Mrs Clifford, his landlady. The room she offered had startled him. However, what did it matter? It was spotlessly clean, as Mrs Calderwood had promised, and at least it was cheerful. Vulgarly cheerful, and Annabel would have had a fit.

The Cliffords' house was one of a working-class terrace sturdily built in red brick about the turn of the century. Hugh had the big front room over the hall and parlour – the best room in the house, Mrs Clifford pointed out. There was a divan bed covered in what the Brookhampton draper labelled 'gay contemporary fabric'. This meant that on a grey background there was a pattern of irregular squares and blobs of red and yellow, with one or two green squiggles to relieve any monotony. The windows were curtained in the same material, while two of the walls were papered in grey with a design of red vases holding yellow daisies. On the other two walls the paper imitated grey stones, and there was a vase of plastic ivy trailing across one of them. Of course, it would catch the dust a bit, Mrs Clifford agreed when displaying the room to her neighbour, but she was prepared to take it down and wash it every week. There were one or two ornaments which astonished Hugh – a crinolined lady, and three pottery birds, of no known species, flying down the wall opposite the ivy.

The room was comfortable, and he soon began to take its appearance for granted. There was a highly varnished oak-veneered sideboard, which he found held all sorts of useful clutter – charts, notebooks, beer bottles – and a vast and overpowering wardrobe with a door which invariably swung open if he trod on a certain floorboard. He soon became adept at avoiding it. There was an easy chair, also covered in the contemporary fabric, and a big old-fashioned gas fire, which gave out a good heat, and had a meter beside it which absorbed shillings and clicked loudly. The floor was covered with highly-polished linoleum imitating parquet – very cold to the feet in the early morning – and two red curly rugs from Woolworth's. In its rather hectic fashion, it was a comfortable-looking room, and after the first shock was over Hugh had little objection to it.

Nicola had. She was horrified. 'How can you live in this frightful place?' she exclaimed. 'You can't go on like this. It's outrageous.'

These remarks were no help.

'I've got to,' he said curtly.

'But surely–' she wailed.

'Surely what?'

'Somebody ought to *do* something,' she complained. 'After all, you know plenty of people. Someone could find you a better job than this, in a less awful – oh, I can't bear it, this is just a ghastly *hole*.'

'You don't have to bear it,' he retorted briefly. Sympathy was what he had longed to receive, not outrage. Outrage – no doubt she meant it kindly, he reminded himself – outrage made him feel much worse. Were things as bad as all this? Perhaps they were, but there was no need to be so dramatic. For the first time she irritated him, but he pushed the thought away.

'It doesn't help to go on about it,' he muttered, and tried to take hold of her warm slight body, that had been so comforting in the past. But she wriggled away, and twitched angrily at the gaudy curtains.

'What are we doing to *do?*' she asked. 'We can't stay *here*.'

He took her to the cinema, though they had both seen the film before, and held despairingly to her hand. Afterwards they had a badly-cooked pompous meal at the grandest hotel in Brookhampton, which cheered her a little. Then he took her to the station and saw her on to her train.

After she had gone he experienced depths of cold futility and desolation. This too had gone wrong. He had counted on her to be his one surety, his consolation, his remaining happiness.

He braced his shoulders firmly. There was no cause for all this despair. It was merely a passing mood. Next weekend he would go up to London to see her, and everything would come right between them. He was wrong to expect her to do the travelling. She had a full-time job. She had been exhausted today, and the whole meeting had been a failure. Small wonder she didn't care for this place. It was drab. Like his life now. She was right. He said so himself. Why had he refused to admit it to her? He had built too much on her visit. He had been longing for the sight of her, the feel of her, his beautiful, fragile Nicola. Somehow it had not occurred to him that she would be affected by the Cliffords' house, by the mean streets. He had thought, he supposed sarcastically, that she would have eyes only for him.

The following week-end she told him she was not free, but a fortnight later he went up to London to see her. This time he made his plans carefully. He arranged to meet her in a bar he knew she liked, he had booked a table for lunch, there was a new exhibition at the Tate which they went to in the afternoon. Then they took a taxi to the Hilton and had tea, another to Soho for dinner, another to the theatre, to the latest John Osborne play.

This was a success. She blossomed for him, and behaved as though there was nothing wrong at all. He repeated the entertainment three weeks later. There was no doubt she appeared to look forward to their meetings. He was reassured, yet dissatisfied. This was not how he had imagined their days together, loaded with trivialities. Where was the rapport that had been between them as they murmured together in the firelight in her big sitting-room, while the record-player surmounted their talk with its triumphant music, modern, discordant, vigorous? They lived only in public now. Their relationship had ceased to be real.

For their next meeting he booked no seats, suggested, after a splendid lunch, that they should go back to her flat for tea. She acquiesced, and he took her there in a taxi.

If possible this was even less satisfactory than their previous meetings. On this occasion, he had to recognise it, the fault was in him. But as soon as they were alone together in her flat he was engulfed in depression. He could not forget how much he had lost, how a brief six months earlier he had been able to take all this for granted, would have left her to go to the busy life of the wards at the Central. Everything had been ahead of him. Now there was only Brookhampton.

He hated Brookhampton. Already, after only a few months there, he hated the place.

Or was it himself he hated?

What sort of man was he, he began to ask? He had suddenly spoilt his own life. Was this bad luck, bad judgement or sheer worthlessness? Now he detested his life. Had he no stamina, no depth, was he able to tolerate nothing but an easy pleasant existence?

This was what his grandfather thought, he knew. Many of them at the Central agreed with him. Why?

Here, of course, they came back to Annabel. This was the conflict. The split between Annabel and his grandfather, the struggle between them during his childhood for possession. They had both been left disappointed. He pleased neither of them.

IV

In Hugh's childhood they had lived at East Callant, in Harbour Cottage, he and Annabel. The cottage was at the bottom of the garden of Harbour House, where at that period the Ravelstons lived in the holidays. Originally, the cottage building had been stables, and later a garage. When Andrew Ravelston had married Annabel, his father had converted it for them, so that they could use it as a weekend cottage. It had its own cosy charm, very different from the cold splendour of Harbour House, which was eighteenth century, high-ceilinged, with enormous sash windows looking out to sea.

Annabel had a gift for making her surroundings reflect her own personality – gay, outgoing, frivolous. In summer, when the yellow front door, which led straight into the low living-room, stood always hospitably open, there were great bowls of roses everywhere, and the room was cool and shadowy, with gay awnings outside the windows, and Annabel herself usually to be found lounging on the big sofa, surrounded by a clutter of magazines, sewing, chocolates, library books. In winter, with the doors closed against the weather, and the warm velvet curtains drawn, the fire burned brightly and lamps shed pools of light. The sofa was drawn up in front of the fire now, Annabel occupied it as usual, with her paraphernalia, and the low table beside it was in Hugh's memory loaded with the silver tea service and the Rockingham china (both wedding presents). Annabel drank pale China tea with lemon. There was the telephone, too, within easy reach. That was another of Hugh's memories. As he grew older, Annabel seemed to spend more time on the telephone.

'But darling, I can't *possibly–*'

'Look, my sweet, you come down here and we'll talk *properly.*'

'My *angel,* how terrible. What *could* you say?'

'Darling, if *only* I could help, you know I wouldn't hesitate for one *minute*. But I am simply *anchored* to this dreadful place, you've no idea.'

'Now, you must positively *promise* me that you're coming down this week-end without fail. I truly can't stand another *minute,* my dear, of these R-r-ravelstons.' Annabel always pronounced the name as though it began with a long French R, an affectation which infuriated Sir Donald Ravelston.

Hugh himself thought it a most wonderful method of pronouncing his name, and practised it carefully, alone in the boat-shed, until he had mastered it.

Unfortunately his skill was not appreciated. To him, it seemed that the heavens fell. He tried it out, first, at school. Miss Gilmour took no apparent notice, though he knew – for he was, even at that age, highly sensitive to the reactions of others – that she disapproved but chose for some reason to say nothing. But his contemporaries not only noticed and shouted at him at the time – 'R-r-ravelston, what do you mean, R-r-ravel-ston? That's not your name, your name's Ravelston.' 'He's bonkers, silly old Ravel-ston's gone bonkers.' 'Rave, rave Ravelston.' 'Ravelston's raving.' It was the joke of the term. 'I say, did you know Ravelston's raving?' 'And frothing at the mouth.' 'See him froth – aren't you frothing, Ravelston?' 'What's your name, then?' 'Hear him froth.'

He had never been set on by the mob before. He stood up to it with fortitude, but he was hurt and astonished, and it taught him a lesson. Next term they had something else to think about, he took care never to pronounce his name again in the way that offended them, and he was received back into favour. But he had learnt to tread warily. He knew how easy it was to put a foot wrong, he knew he had to be careful not to put himself outside the pale. That was only one of the lessons he learnt from the episode. The second was that in the outside world it was unsafe to trust his mother's guidance. What she did was often mistaken. Home was one thing, outside was another.

He was about six when he found this out, and from then on life had been conflict or compromise. It hadn't, he realised later, been easy for Annabel. Beautiful, respon-sive, gay, she had been widowed at only twenty-two, left in the midst of the serious Ravelstons with her small son. She had been forced to live in Harbour Cottage – which until then had been their week-end home only – since she had no money. Sir Donald Ravelston gave her an allowance, she had a small, rapidly dwindling, amount of capital from Andrew's insurance, and that was all. Her father-in-law had promised to make himself responsible for Hugh's education.

At first, lonely and bereft, she turned all her attention to looking after Hugh and being a pathetic widow. She went up to Harbour House and talked to Sir Donald Ravelston, who, while hardly taken in by her, nevertheless enjoyed these sessions in which she made much of him. Few men could resist Annabel when she turned her charm on. Later, though, they actively disliked one another. Annabel grew tired of putting herself out for her father-in-law, stuffy old curmudgeon, and he grew increasingly irritated by her affectations.

Annabel began to complain to her son. 'Your grandfather is impossible.' 'I suppose you'd better show up at Harbour House for Sunday lunch as usual, but I simply can't face it myself. All those tedious Ravelstons, talking all the time about drugs or boats – you must say I'm lying down with a headache.' 'Thank heavens the Ravelstons are nothing to do with me, except by the accident of marriage. Your father was the *only* tolerable member of that *ghastly* family.'

In time the complaints became accusations. 'What are you doing, sitting there with your nose in a book? Don't tell me *you're* turning into a typical Ravelston.' 'Don't look at me like that, *say* something, can't you? Answer me, Hugh, I tell you, answer me. I won't have you behaving like one of those awful Ravelstons, all buttoned up and full of complexes.' She longed for some response. She wanted him to scream back at her.

The trouble was, he couldn't. He could never bear to fight with her, to do so made him cold throughout his bones. Annabel loved rows, they invigorated her, they renewed her confidence in herself.

'I won't have you going about keeping that stiff upper lip like a horrible Ravelston,' she urged him for his own good. 'Spit it out, my darling, don't bottle it up inside you. Tell Mummie, my darling. I only want to help you. What *is* it, my pet?'

But he made himself stiff and silent in her loving embrace, though at other times he longed for the comfort of her arms. But when she made these frantic demands on him, somewhere he shrivelled and fled. She felt that he had rejected her, and blamed the Ravelstons. Was this the baby she had borne and nursed, who had been all hers? Was it for this aloof little creature she had buried herself down at East Callant?

'You're nothing but a Ravelston,' she

declared bitterly when most enraged by him. 'Let me tell you, you'll live to regret it. They're all hard and cold, they're just walking books, and that's what you're turning into, only I won't let you.' She must save him from himself.

'You're pedantic, nothing but a stuck-up know-all, like all the Ravelstons. You think you're so clever, passing your exams, and coming first. Let me tell you, Mr Clever, there are other things in life than passing exams, and it's time you found out about them. You won't find out by looking in your precious books, either.'

She was jealous of his books. He was too young to understand this, but she had been jealous of Andrew's interest in medicine, jealous of anything that took him away from her. Now it had all dwindled to jealousy of the books her son read, that would lead him along the road his father had followed, the road the Ravelstons trod so sanctimoniously. Her jealousy led not only to major quarrels, but also to petty upsets. If Hugh went to his room to do his homework, she followed him there, demanding to know what he wanted for his supper, whether he liked the arrangement of flowers she had made for his bedside table, if he approved of her new hat. If he sat in their sitting-room, reading, she constantly interrupted him. She was never so talkative as when he had a book in his hands, moving the flowers to fifteen different places and asking his opinion on each, giving him a cushion he didn't want, changing the position of the lamp so that it gave him a better light and then standing between it and his book, talking and playing with the tassel of the cushion she had insisted on stuffing behind his unwilling back, asking him what was on the radio, was the clock slow, when was he going to mow the lawn for her, would he fetch some more logs, and while he was up, could he see her scissors anywhere. Perhaps she had left them upstairs, would he be an angel and go and see?

He was not an angel and he wouldn't go and see. She was desolate. Other people didn't have children like this. Other people had well-behaved, kind and thoughtful children, only too eager to run little errands for their mothers. He was a typical Ravelston, thinking only of himself and his own boring pursuits. Selfish, cold, aloof. 'One day you'll realise you haven't any friends left, and it'll be all your own fault. People are beginning to notice how stodgy you are.'

'Well, what about you?' he would in the end, goaded, shout. 'What about you? Do you think you're so perfect yourself?'

She took refuge, always, in hurt motherhood. 'How can you speak to me like this, after all I've done? Other people's children don't speak to their mothers like this, other people–'

'Other mothers aren't like you,' he retorted, but with how much truth he was unaware. He loved her dearly, and loathed quarrelling with her. He hated her to disapprove of him. Most of all, he hated her to disapprove of him for being a Ravelston. Because always there were these two main streams of feeling possessing him. One was his love for her, and the other his passion for all the Ravelstons at Harbour House, his grandfather, Uncle Archie, his cousins, Rodney and Don. He worshipped them, and all their activities. He longed to become part of their splendid adult life.

This was hard on Annabel, who had, in addition to a jealous nature, something to be jealous about. It was hard, too, for an unknowing young Ravelston, growing up in the cottage at the bottom of the garden, looking both ways, his heart in both houses.

Hard for him, too, was the fact that his grandfather disliked him. In childhood he had not known this, had tried always to please the old man, had recognised that he seldom succeeded, but had constantly hoped for a better result. But the truth was that Sir Donald Ravelston had become obsessed with his dislike of Annabel and all her ways. He disapproved of her, and he disapproved of what she was making of his youngest grandson. To remember his son Andrew saddened him. To think that this was all that was left of him, this silly girl and the disappointing little boy, was unbearable. He recognised, though, that there was little he could do about it. He would not descend to squabbling with Annabel over the boy. That would do no good to anyone. With typical Ravelston disengagement, he turned his interest deliberately to his son Archie's children, Rodney and Don, and wrote Hugh off as a dead loss. But he could not so easily control the sense of failure and irritation that overcame him when he met Hugh – who, understandably, bore all the surface signs of Annabel's upbringing, and was a somewhat affected and supercilious little boy, very different from Archie and Jean's two young ruffians. The Ravelstons thought Hugh effeminate and precious. When one holiday, Don, who had a caustic wit and who had newly returned from Garside self-consciously sophisticated, remarked at the breakfast table 'and what about the fairy at the bottom of our garden? Is he – or she – included in the party? Or will it be too rough for her?' not only was he not rebuked, but the remark was an enormous success with his grandfather, who laughed more heartily than he had been known to do for years.

So the nickname stuck. Hugh was the fairy at the bottom of the garden as far as Don and all his friends were concerned. When Hugh went to Garside a year later, the nickname preceded him. At first he had been too young to comprehend Don's meaning, and thought he was being mocked as a pretty aerial creature from the book of fairy stories Annabel had read to him when he was younger. He had been hurt and offended by the nickname then, but when he went to Garside and its full meaning painfully began to dawn on him, he had been almost beside himself with rage and horror. He was not like that at all. He had a great many fights on his hands, for the label took a lot of living down. He never forgave Don for it.

That he was able to live it down he owed, he had always considered, to Rodney. Of all the Ravelstons, Rodney was the closest to him. He took the place of father and elder brother. Rodney led him from the bright little mother's darling that he had undoubtedly been at five or six to the thirteen-year-old who had been tough enough to follow Don to Garside and make a place for himself despite the reputation Don had given him. Rodney taught Hugh to row and then to sail – despite Annabel – supervised his early days afloat, and, to his terrified delight, first let him handle the sails of his International 14 foot under instruction, but eventually allowed him to take the helm for brief periods. Rodney was one of those instinctive helmsmen who can feel the wind on the sails in the palm of their hands, and he shouted furiously to Hugh if he failed to keep the boat on the wind.

Annabel was always in a bad temper when they returned from sailing. Hugh had usually dodged her when he left to join Rodney, so there would be trouble about that, trouble because he had been sailing, and more trouble because he was almost invariably late for some meal. Annabel would be angry with Rodney, too, but Rodney, to Hugh's vast admiration, appeared imperturbable.

Hugh was doubly guilty on these occasions, in Annabel's bad books himself, and the cause of Rodney's ticking off, in addition. He would apologise profusely. 'Not to worry,' Rodney would answer comfortably. 'What's the odds? The grown-ups are always on about something or other. It doesn't matter.' Rodney was a great one for going his own way, and he almost succeeded in teaching Hugh to ignore Annabel's displeasure.

Those sailing days of childhood remained golden in his memory. Those were the days when his friendship with Rodney had begun. Until then, Rodney had been his admired elder cousin, to be worshipped from a distance only. But from the day when Rodney first gave him the oars and patiently instructed him in rowing, a friendship grew. There were seven years between them, but from the time Hugh was eight until he went to Garside at thirteen, he was, during the long holidays, Rodney's shadow. The affection was not one-sided. They became devoted to one another. When Hugh went to Garside they drifted apart, because by this time Rodney was at Cambridge and the busy years began for him, first his degree, then medical studies at the Central, then his house jobs. No more long holidays at East Callant for Rodney, though when he was there, Hugh would drop everything, offend anyone to crew for him.

This, Hugh thought now at Brookhampton, during his painful self-examination, this at least was genuine. His friendship with Rodney – there had been no element of display here, nothing phony.

What about sailing, though? Had he struggled to succeed in this merely to impress Rodney and his grandfather? Or had he enjoyed it for its own sake?

Did he do anything for its own sake?

Trying to be honest, trying not to give himself the benefit of any doubt, he decided that his love of the sea and sailing had been sincere. He had loved both the skill and the excitement of sailing, the freedom of the sea when he sailed his dinghy alone, singing to himself in the wide estuary, or disturbing the ducks up the broad river reaches, hearing the fish plop and the water slap the hull. He had loved the holidays on *Moon Maid,* old Donald Ravelston's *Vertue,* and later the companionship of cruising and racing *Opening Snap,* the hospital sailing club's *Pionier.* He enjoyed the hard days in Force 6 and 7, the struggle to reef or change the sail, the hot meal afterwards in the crowded cabin, the good talk in the cockpit under the stars. Racing *Opening Snap* was a hard life, but a satisfying one. Sailing meant beauty and friendship and hardship surmounted.

But he knew to his disgust that he had loved too the impression he made. Hugh Ravelston as he had always longed to be, tough, popular, successful, self-assured.

Before he went to Garside, even, when he was at his prep school, Annabel had remarried. This had been no surprise to anyone but Hugh, and he, polite, reserved, every inch a Ravelston, as Annabel thought despairingly, had shown nothing of what he felt. For months, years even, he had seen that his life with Annabel was dwindling to nothing. He had forced himself to deny his fears. For the past couple of years, though, Jean had often appeared on speech day, Jean had collected him at the end of term and driven him down to Harbour House. 'I'm not sure,' she had increasingly often said, 'if Annabel is down at the cottage yet. Stay and have tea with us, Hugh, and then you can pop down and see if she's arrived.' Only too often she hadn't. Then there might or might not be a telephone call, and Jean might tell him Annabel had been held up. He must stay the night at Harbour House. Often he had stayed for over a week, and Annabel had opened the cottage for only ten days or so of the holiday. Then she married again, someone called Simon Crowther. Hugh knew he himself would never count for anything in her life again.

It wasn't that he didn't like Simon. Simon was always tremendously friendly. But he and Annabel were a pair. Soon they had babies, too. Hugh, as he had suspected would be the case from the beginning, had no part in their life. He was no more than a visitor. He didn't even much enjoy the holidays he spent with them. Annabel was busy, although she had an *au pair* girl to help her, the babies were all over the place all day, and in the evening Annabel and Simon's smart friends took over. It was a polished life, with a good deal of name-dropping, and he was a stranger in it. Frequently, he preferred to take refuge at Harbour House, where there was always a welcome from Jean, if not from the old man.

By the time he was fourteen, Harbour House had become his home. The old intimate days at the cottage had vanished. Useless to try to deceive himself. Annabel had lost interest in him.

Each holiday he faced this fact with cold despair. Because somehow each term he did manage to deceive himself, to persuade himself that it had all been his own fault, he was, as Annabel constantly pointed out, a cold and unresponsive Ravelston. Next holidays would be different. He was older, now, he had matured this term, he understood far more. Next hols he would be different. He would show Annabel how much she meant to him. They would somehow get back on the old footing.

Of course, they never did. Soon, Annabel ceased even to come to Harbour Cottage. Simon found a post with UNESCO and they made their home in Switzerland. This was the exotic life Annabel had longed for when she had been, as she always described it, 'buried down at the cottage, miles from anywhere, with that awful old man in Harbour House looking down his nose at me.'

Hugh used to join them for short holidays. Annabel asserted that he expanded during these periods away from England and the Ravelstons. Certainly he showed a different facet of himself when he joined their circle. But by this time he was so unmistakably a Ravelston that he could not join it for long. He had too many commitments at home. Rugger, cricket, climbing, sailing – he was in demand for all these activities, to join touring teams, play in matches, instruct at

Outward Bound schools, on CCPR courses, crew in races. He genuinely lacked the time to join Annabel for more than a week or two, once or twice a year.

These holidays, though, he had enjoyed. He had often wished he could stay longer. For Annabel, now, began once more to make a fuss of him. He was her handsome and distinguished eldest son, who had won prizes, a cricket blue, played rugger for the hospital, did interesting things and won honours in all directions – Annabel was not clear what they all signified, but she knew Hugh had achievements behind him that earned him respect and admiration when people heard about them. He reflected great credit on her.

Then, too, people were always amazed that she could have a son of his age, and it was pleasant to astonish them, to receive congratulations on her looks. To do her justice, Annabel was not the type to pretend to be younger than she was. Blonde and sophisticated, slim, with huge speaking brown eyes, she was a charmer now as she had always been. But she enjoyed basking in the cries of surprise and amazement.

'Well, darling, I did marry frightfully young, I know – I was only nineteen when I had Hugh, after all – but let's face it, I'm forty now.'

'Annabel, you simply *can't* be. You don't

look a day over thirty, honestly.' And she didn't. Simon, now, looked a haggard fifty. Dominic and Sebastian – 'Dominic and now *Sebastian*, really, how typically affected of Annabel,' the Ravelstons had chorused disgustedly. 'Poor little beasts,' they had added. 'Imagine having to live *that* down at Garside.' 'Don't suppose they'll have to live it down,' the old man had pointed out. 'She won't send them to Garside – she didn't want Hugh to go.' 'No, they'll go to some cranky school abroad,' Rodney agreed, 'where everybody is called Sebastian or Gabriel – the ones who'll get it taken out of them will be the ones called John or George.' Annabel's two younger sons, in fact, both had a worried, elderly look in repose. Annabel herself was flourishing. At last she had the life she longed for. Away from dreary old England, the dull old medical Ravelstons, to a country where the sun often shone, where everywhere was clean, where you could still get maids, where the climate had proper seasons, snow in winter, alpine flowers in spring, heavenly summer, autumn crocus on the slopes before the days drew in, and where she could live in a circle of *cultured* people.

Annabel had gone overboard for culture. For years now she had attended art galleries, concerts, lectures, play readings. She had entertained visiting English writers, dons, musicians, even headmasters and bishops –

though she found these slightly sticky going, reminiscent of the Ravelstons, in fact – with charm and grace. She was a great help to Simon. Now she claimed acquaintance with well-known names, and had many friends who existed precariously on the outskirts of Bohemia.

She often thought Hugh could have been an actor. He was so good looking, and he had great feeling for poetry and drama – or he used to have, before he went to that horrible Garside, and learnt to hide his emotions, she confided sadly on numerous occasions. He had always had beautiful bones, and a transforming smile – 'I flatter myself that he is not wholly Ravelston. There are some qualities he has from *me*,' she would add here. 'He would look magnificent on the screen,' she asserted hopefully.

Nothing came of this. As it turned out, Annabel was not sorry. She liked to have her handsome, distinguished son, who was a doctor at the Central London Hospital, to display. A visitor from another world, she would announce proudly, as though she had managed to secure a baby elephant or a Martian on her travels.

Annabel couldn't quite understand what had happened about Hugh's career. He had come out to spend Christmas, looking quite dreadful, with some long story, so that she had been quite worried, for a time. But he soon seemed to cheer up, and she decided that he had simply been exhausted, that was all there was to it. He *would* work too hard, of course – hadn't she always said so?

He told her he had had to leave the Central, she was quite clear about that. Well, it was a horrid stuffy old place, full of dreary old fogies like Sir Donald Ravelston. Perhaps he could go somewhere a bit more enterprising now, go-ahead, like that marvellous clinic for instance, where Marie-Paul had had that wonderful operation – in Zurich, was it? Or what about that Bircher-Benner place, where they knew all sorts of fascinating things about food? Or perhaps Bad-Gastein – hadn't someone said the waters there were radio-active? Surely that would interest him? Anyway, there must be a tremendous number of exciting possibilities. The Central wasn't the only place in the world. There was no need at all to stay in England.

Hugh pointed out that he could no longer practise medicine, that his name was not on the register. She couldn't see why not. He'd passed all his exams, hadn't he? They couldn't take that away, could they? He explained it all to her. But she was unworried, for she read no suffering in his face when he told her.

Here she was right. Telling Annabel – except, of course, that he had totally failed to get the situation over to her – had been far from difficult. Hilarious, would be nearer the truth. The ironical Ravelston sense of humour had risen uncontrollably during their conversation – which would have caused Sir Donald Ravelston's hair to stand on end, so strange were the assumptions Annabel made on the subject of medicine. For the first time Hugh was genuinely amused as he told his dismal tale. Annabel's incomprehension was so complete, her bafflement so sincere, that he suddenly saw his own world in a new perspective. He smiled tolerantly as much at his own agonies as at her rose-coloured spectacles.

'Just a lot of silly old stupids,' she remarked encouragingly. 'You don't want to pay any attention to them, darling. You just go ahead and *show* them. I know you can.'

'Show them what?' he asked gently. 'It's a bit difficult, you know, to – er – show the G.M.C. where it gets off.'

'Show them,' she cried in ringing tones, 'show them you're a Ravelston.'

He exploded into gales of relaxing laughter. Annabel was most offended.

'After all, you *are* a Ravelston,' she pointed out, as though he might have overlooked the fact. 'Darling Andrew was a Ravelston, and so of course are you. The Ravelstons,' she added triumphantly, 'are *most* distinguished.'

Hugh snorted again. 'A dreary lot of old fogies,' he reminded her.

'Oh, of course they're *dreadfully* boring,' she agreed at once. 'Nobody – but *nobody* – can possibly know that better than I do. I can't *tell* you how I suffered when you were a little boy, and I was simply stuck there, in that benighted place, with no one to talk to but Ravelstons. You can absolutely have not the slightest conception how ghastly it was.'

She was right. He had not. He wondered momentarily how she would react if he told her that at Brookhampton he had found no one to talk to, not even Ravelstons. He began to try to give her some idea of his life there, but she soon interrupted him.

'Why *stay* there, darling? Why don't you live here with us? You know I'd *adore* it. You could look round and find yourself some nice job, with civilised people. Anyway, there's no hurry. You could just stay here, and talk to me – take me about, that would be lovely. Have a really good holiday, for once, not simply a miserable week, which is all I ever seem to get you for. Why don't you, darling? There's nothing I'd like better, and after all, you needn't be bored. There's skiing now, and swimming and climbing later on. You could even get a boat and sail on the lake, if you can't live without one, though I'd rather you didn't of course. But there'd be plenty for you to do. You seem to me to have been working far too hard for years and years.'

Why didn't he stay? What she said was true. Why stodge away in Brookhampton? Why not live abroad with Annabel, enjoying, as she suggested, climbing and swimming, good Swiss coffee and black cherry jam for breakfast, aperitifs at pavement cafés, lively talk until late in the night, wonderful food, wonderful climate, dramatic mountain views, music, dancing, lovely girls in *après-ski* wear – lovely *après-ski*, in fact. And always the busy pleasant social life, the visiting celebrities, the dinners, the mountain picnics in alpine meadows in summer, the ski-ing parties in winter.

Was he mad to turn it all down?

In the past he had always enjoyed life with Annabel in Switzerland, it had been so different from Harbour House, or the hospital, it had been a glorious break with routine, a gay world of happy irresponsibility. He had loved to drop into it and savour its delights.

But it had never been a way of life. Or not for him, though undoubtedly it was for Annabel and Simon. Presumably he was too much a Ravelston for it. What a confession, he thought wryly. He must be too stuffy and pompous, too serious-minded in exactly the heavy humourless way that Annabel so much deplored, to be able to enjoy light-hearted pleasures. For him, he supposed, life had to have a purpose. Annabel's existence was trivial. Very pleasant for a brief holiday, for recreation, but nothing to do with the real business of living. It was not, he thought suddenly, a man's world at all.

This, of course, was to echo his grandfather's views. He had always considered the old man's attitude to Annabel's world to be ridiculously prejudiced and bigoted. Now he found himself looking through his eyes, seeing as he did.

This was a fine time to discover he shared his grandfather's opinions. A thoroughly inconvenient, awkward time to look at life through Ravelston eyes. But he knew this was, for him at least, truth. He had made his choice. He preferred to be a Ravelston, even when it profited him nothing. Back to the Brookhampton job, and the daily grind.

V

During this miserable time in Brookhampton, Hugh Ravelston came to know himself – to know himself, and not to like himself. He understood a great deal that he had never grasped before.

He blamed himself, now, not only for the past, but for the present. He had slipped into isolation. He had been aloof from them all in the laboratory, aloof from Jock Calderwood, he had cut himself off from friends in London. He joined in no Brookhampton activity, and abstained from all he had done during his Central days. This was to a certain extent inevitable. He had played rugger for the Central, for instance, and been Secretary of the Central Sailing Club. But he could have played rugger for the Brookhampton General, he could have sailed with the Calderwoods – Jock Calderwood's boat was moored in the estuary, within sight of his study window. Hugh knew, too, that he would have been welcome at many evenings with his own group at the Central. They would never have thrown him out. But they were too busy and pressed for time to seek him out, to pursue him when he turned down their first conscientious invitations. They had other things on their minds.

Only Ben ignored his rebuffs, travelled down to Brookhampton whenever he could find a spare day, dragged him out to the Calderwoods' house and took him sailing or walking over the marshes. Through Ben's efforts he was forced into friendship with Jock Calderwood, with whom he had tried to adopt an attitude of rigid formality once he was on his staff.

Slowly he was beginning to work through his difficulties, ceasing to point the finger of scorn at himself, preparing to take up every-day life again. Concentration was returning, he began to be able to work through the day without lapsing into memories, to read biochemistry in the evenings without drifting into regrets.

Before he had established himself firmly in the present, though, he had to take another knock, which jolted him out of his precarious acceptance of reality. For some months he had seen little of Nicola. He knew the life he could offer her was dull, and he had made no attempt to tie her down. But he had always longed, of course, in spite of himself, that she would demonstrate her devotion to him, no matter what he asked.

He soon came to understand that she was going round with friends of his at the Central. He forced himself to accept this. What did he expect her to do, sit in her flat and knit? It was a blow, though. For the first time in his life he had to grasp that a beautiful girl might not find him good value. He had only himself to offer, and this was not enough. No Alfa-Romeo, no gay life, no promising career as a future consultant at the Central. Yet he had thought she had genuinely loved him. She had seemed to do so. But down at Brookhampton he had watched her love steadily evaporating, as his prospects died. Had she deliberately deceived him, pretending to care for him, while after only what he had to offer? He knew himself wiser now, sardonic and worldly, disillusioned. This was all it had been, and he had fallen for it. Sucker. He was well out of that.

Yet he could not let himself quite accept this. Here was one more conflict, one more torturing indecision to plague his days and nights. He abandoned himself now to imagining that she had never loved him, now to blaming himself for doubting her love. Always he longed to hold her in his arms, as he had so often done in the old days. If only things turned out to be all right between them, if only he could have her back, feel her warmth, her supple body, hold her, at least, safely to him. Comfort could have been found with her, and with no one else. Without her he was alone.

Well, there it was, he was alone. She was out when he telephoned, her conversation was evasive, she put him off when he tried to meet her. He was not surprised, though he felt more bereft and alone than he had ever been, when she became engaged – to someone at the Central, of course. What did astonish him, knocked him sideways, was that she proposed to marry his cousin Don. He felt this was almost the worst blow of all. She had left him for Don. He could not see how to deal with this.

It was Ben who told him, Ben who came down and stayed for the week-end. But after Ben had gone back to London, the loneliness began again, worse than ever before, complete, engulfing. There was nothing left now. It was all over, all gone. Rule it off and turn over the page.

There was disillusion too. Nicola's love had been a sham, based on what he had to offer her materially. He had trusted her love, but in fact there had been nothing there. It was pointless even to regret her loss – though he did, constantly – because in reality there could have been no love between them. If there had been, she could never have left him like this, for Don.

And so the slow months passed in Brookhampton, the days grew longer. A mist of green caught the light among the trees, and Mrs Clifford put a jar of daffodils on his window sill. Soon in the small front garden a stunted lilac came into bloom, scenting the petrol-laden air with a promise of summer.

In April, Rodney's letter came, out of a silence that had hurt Hugh more than he dared to admit. This marked the turning point. The knowledge that Rodney had not, after all, written him off like their grandfather filled Hugh with a sudden surge of energy, of renewed faith in the future, ended the inertia that had been poisoning him.

Rodney's letter had other, more tangible, results. He lent Hugh *Sea Goose*. Writing from the base in the Antarctic, Rodney had longed to be able to help Hugh in some way.

But there had seemed nothing that he could do. Nothing that he could write in a letter could come between Hugh and his changed circumstances.

One action, though, he could take. As soon as he thought of it, he knew it was inevitable.

Rodney Ravelston had one great love, his boat, *Sea Goose*. He dreamed about her. He had, more than once, put her needs before the demands even of his work, certainly of Emma and the children. She led a secret life in his soul, was part of his hidden inner life.

When he first heard the news about Hugh, Rodney had written to Emma, asking for facts. She had supplied these, worse than he had expected, and had told him that Hugh was now working in Brookhampton. 'You'd think it was the jungle, from the way they all talk,' she had reported.

Rodney wrote at once to Hugh, and also to the yard at East Callant, where *Sea Goose* was laid up. He told Hugh to collect *Sea Goose* and sail her himself.

This had been all he had been able to offer in the way of comfort to a young cousin in disgrace, and he had no hesitation, only regret at the inadequacy of his support. Later, as the months wore by, he was to suffer torments of anxiety. Hugh was a senseless boy, no more. What if he set light to her – he'd quite likely go ashore one day leaving the gas on. He had not the faintest idea of maintenance. She'd probably be dismasted, he'd over-canvas her to win some damn fool race, and tear the guts out of her.

His grandfather did nothing to allay his anxiety. 'What possessed you to let that young fool have *Sea Goose?*' he wrote angrily from East Callant. He had heard, of course, from the yard what was happening. He refused to meet Hugh, but he watched his departure through binoculars from the landing window, cursing and grumbling and going downstairs to telephone Archie with the news. His housekeeper – Mrs Penman, a former patient who had become his parlour-maid thirty years earlier, had married his chauffeur, and now, with her husband, looked after him in the cottage – had been amused and delighted. 'That's stirred the doctor up all right,' she announced at supper that night. 'On to Mr Archie like a flash, he was, that's given him something to think about. He's got his charts out now, doing all that plotting, round to the Brook-hampton river, where young Hugh's taking her. Cross as two sticks, he is, but lively as a cartload of monkeys.' It was her somewhat narrow view that Hugh's misdeeds did the doctor – she had never learnt to call him Sir Donald, or Archie the Professor, it was doubtful if she believed in him as such – a world of good, and made him more like his

103

old self.

Sir Donald Ravelston expected the worst, and told Rodney so. The family had been forbidden to write to Rodney about Hugh's disaster, in case they should worry him, but the old man had no hesitation whatever in trying to alarm him about the fate of *Sea Goose*. *That careless boy*, he wrote in a long letter to Rodney, *will undoubtedly* ... there followed a catalogue of all the catastrophes the old man had been able to conjure up ... *have a collision, leave the gas on, let rust get into the engine, dismast her.* Worst of all, he ended, *he has not the faintest notion of the hard work you have to put into maintenance.*

Rodney wrote furiously back to say that all this was nonsense, and went on worrying more than ever.

If he had been able to see Hugh's reactions, he would have known his gesture worth any twinges of anxiety he might experience. Rodney's permission to sail *Sea Goose* altered Hugh's days out of all recognition. No longer was he, in the evenings, kicking his heels, lonely and miserable, in his room at Malden Road, trying unsuccessfully to read biochemistry as an antidote to despair. As soon as Rodney's letter came, he was plunged into activity. He had to find moorings. He sought Jock Calderwood's advice, and followed up his suggestions. He rang up the yard at East Callant to arrange about fitting out. He bought new charts, and pored over them. There was hardly time enough to brush up on his navigation – which had never been a strong point – before she was in the water.

He telephoned Ben, who had promised to take a week-end to bring *Sea Goose* round from East Callant to Brookhampton. Ben was unable to manage the first week-end Hugh suggested, but he could do the second. The postponement turned out to be useful, since Hugh utilised it to travel to East Callant himself, and go over *Sea Goose* with loving care, checking and making her ready for the trip, and provisioning her. He slept on board – he would have done anyway, for he was filled with far too much excitement to have gone ashore, but in fact he was not offered a bed at Harbour Cottage. His grandfather ignored his letter telling him that he was visiting East Callant, and cleared off to stay with Archie for the week-end.

A week later, Hugh and Ben sailed on the evening tide, soon after their arrival at East Callant. To sail into the night with Ben, himself the skipper – however temporary – of *Sea Goose*. This was living again.

Hugh had always loved night sailing. He loved the mystery, the promise, the beauty. Sailing at night was so remote from daily routine as to give the illusion, briefly, of having gained another world. The added spice of danger provided exhilaration.

Then there was Ben's steady presence, and the awareness that, whatever happened to his career, he still had this old enduring friendship, tried and proven, and valued now as perhaps never before. Hugh had shared his misery with Ben, and this had added a new strength to their friendship. There was little now hidden from Ben, who had seen him at his lowest ebb, and who had remained unalterably there, rocklike, filled with common sense. 'No use recriminating,' he had said more than once, as Hugh had poured out his misery, his self-scorn, his despair, his rage, his longing somehow to turn the clock back – this futile longing, that clung to him still, to undo the past. 'What's done can't be undone,' Ben had maintained. Trite but true, and it needed saying, for Hugh knew it, yet could seldom accept its finality. 'Perhaps you've been a fool,' he would go on. 'Well, of *course* you've been a fool. But aren't we all, off and on? And we don't have to pay this price. But there it is, you're faced with it, you've got to pay up and look pleasant.' This had all been in the early days, when Hugh was tearing himself to pieces with regret and conflict, with a hopelessly mistaken belief that with sufficient will-power he could alter the facts. 'You've just got to live through this stage,' Ben had said firmly, when his case was coming up and it all hung in the balance. 'No good trying to see what can be salvaged.

Don't wear yourself out trying. Just live through it as best you can.' Mundane, undramatic advice, but sound. Together they had lived through it.

They were still together, sailing *Sea Goose* on a moonlit sea, though now it was Ben who had the world before him, his career at the Central mapped out, his future assured, and Hugh whose life appeared to lie in the byways of mediocrity. This was not what had been forecast.

At Garside, later at Cambridge, and then at the Central, Ben had been considered a very ordinary chap. Reliable, of course, and no fool. But undistinguished. What had never been ordinary about him was his sterling goodness of heart. Ben had never been known to let anyone down. In addition, he was exceptionally competent. Not brilliant, or inspired, but enormously capable. They had thought him plodding, but now all this competence and reliability, coupled with his recognisably kind nature, was going to add up to a distinguished career. This was somewhat of a surprise to a number of people, particularly his contemporaries.

It was a surprise to Hugh. It would have been a surprise even if he had been there alongside Ben, with an equally distinguished career opening out. But to find that they had changed places – this made him think hard.

Ben deserved success. It was impossible to deny this. He was a capable physician, and would be as much a source of strength to his patients as he had always been to Hugh. He had integrity, and this, of course, was far more rare a quality than they had imagined, in the idealistic untried days at school and university.

That he could ever be shown up as discernably inferior to Ben had never previously occurred to Hugh. But now he could not evade seeing that this was the case. The most that could be said for him was that he might just about amount to a very ordinary chap. A very ordinary chap who had had a lot of bad luck, and who hadn't had the least notion of how to cope with it. And even the bad luck would never have come his way – after all, nothing like it had come Ben's way, had it? – if he had not more or less asked for it. Don had been right all these years. He was a rotten little show-off.

All he could do when things went wrong was to feel sorry for himself, regret his lost opportunities, despise his new colleagues, despise Brookhampton, despise anything it offered – sit about sulking, in fact. A spoilt child.

He had imagined, in his egotism, that he could do this inferior job with one hand tied behind his back and his thoughts elsewhere. Dull routine, no more. He had slammed through the essential duties of his day in a lackadaisical, couldn't care less manner. He must be a liability to Calderwood. Any keen young technician could have done as much, and would have been a more pleasant personality to have around the place. He had been disagreeable, and thoroughly unco-operative. He must snap out of it, make the best of a bad job, not the worst. Be civil. Come out from his murky mood, and, if he had troubles, at least cease to force everyone else to suffer from them.

Too late to go round ingratiating himself with his colleagues. They avoided him now, except for essential conversations. He would have to live that down. But it was not too late to immerse himself in his work, to throw himself into its details, to consider its implications – to do the job properly.

He began to do this, and was surprised how much it helped him in other ways. He found satisfaction in work again, became genuinely more good-humoured. Traces of the Ravelston wit – hitherto unknown to them at the Brookhampton General – appeared spontaneously from time to time. He became a tolerable person to live with.

In the evenings and at week-ends he sailed *Sea Goose,* or pottered about aboard, seeing to the infinitesimal details of her care. He found, now that he was totally responsible for her, that there was a great deal to do.

Hardly time to sail, in fact, he told Calderwood one day with grin, by the time he had done the navigation, got stores on board, checked over the engine, made the sails ready. 'Soon I shall be one of those sailors who never put to sea – too busy.'

Soon the summer was nearly over. Calderwood's research project was completed and written up. It was now in typescript, and once the figures had received their final checking would be sent off for publication. There was only the clearing up to be done. The holiday season was still on though, and the laboratory was understaffed, so Hugh turned his hand to almost anything that needed doing, and learnt a good deal in the process.

Now he came to know Colin Warr. He had seen him about the hospital, of course. Warr was a big-framed, rugged looking man, blunt-featured, with washed-out blue eyes and sparse greying hair, who made an impact wherever he went. He was the junior consultant in general medicine at the hospital.

The first time Hugh was introduced to him, though, was at the Calderwoods. Afterwards he saw that this meeting had been planned by Jock Calderwood for a purpose, but at the time he had been taken off his guard.

'Come out for a meal this evening,' Calderwood had said casually. The technicians had left, and they had the laboratory to themselves. They had been checking the tables for Calderwoods' paper. 'No need to change – I'll run you out.' He took him aboard *Sea Spray* before they went into the house. She was moored out in the estuary, which stretched wide and gleaming on three sides of the Calderwood's sprawling old farmhouse on the marshes, with its casement windows wide to the wind from the sea. They both enjoyed themselves listening to what Jock Calderwood asserted to be a new noise from the diesel, which they eventually traced and remedied. Then they returned, grimy and satisfied, to the house, and found Colin Warr already there.

This was the first occasion on which a visit to the Calderwoods had involved Hugh in meeting one of the consultant staff at the Brookhampton General, and he flinched at the encounter. For all his recent resolution, he remained raw from the pain of rejection from medicine, and he was ill at ease still with unknown members of what he could not help thinking of as his own profession. He had not learnt how to handle the situation. He knew no half-way house between keeping silent and letting them assume he had had no medical training – a procedure which had proved disastrous in the pathology laboratory, and which he was loath to repeat – or laying the fact that he had been struck off the medical register before them as an embarrassing challenge.

Now in Jock Calderwood's study, while sherry was being poured, the difficult decision had to be taken. He could not embark on deception again. On the other hand, he must not, he told himself vehemently, make a scene or let Calderwood down in any way. After a brief introduction, Warr said, 'You're working in the path lab, are you?'

'Yes,' Hugh said, and paused. It ought to come now, some sort of statement, before the moment had gone. 'Dr Calderwood found me a job,' he began with difficulty.

At this point Colin Warr came to life. 'Found him a job' – why had he needed one found for him? Being Colin Warr, there was no tactful hanging back until more information emerged. *'Found* you a job?' he repeated. 'Why? Did you need one so badly?'

'Yes. I did. I–' the words came slowly. He was feeling his way between truth and over-much drama, for one thing, and in any case he had to force the damning phrases into existence. 'I – I was trained as a physician,' he said, and paused to gather himself together for the ultimate fact.

'Were you?' Warr's face was surprised. 'Where?' he asked unexpectedly.

'Cambridge and the Central London,' Hugh said briefly. These details were getting in the way, when he was trying to make matters clear.

Warr looked even more surprised. This was apparent. After all, medical graduates from Cambridge and the Central London are not normally to be found doing odd jobs in provincial hospital laboratories.

Calderwood materialised with glasses of sherry, and overheard the last sentences. He took a hand himself. 'Hugh is not practising at present,' he remarked. The understatement of the year, as far as Hugh was concerned. 'He's not on the register,' he added, as though this were some minor quirk of personal choice.

Hugh had been about to take a sip of sherry, but this was going too far. He threw back his head and looked down the Ravelston nose. 'Struck off is the more usual way of expressing the position,' he explained in a voice of ice, and spilt his sherry on to his trousers. Damn, now he was making a scene after all. He took out his handkerchief and mopped irritably.

'What for?' Warr asked simply.

Hugh found this a relief. Back to facts. 'Manslaughter mainly,' he said. 'But–' he explained about Angela Carlton.

Warr made no comment, but asked 'What were you doing before all this happened?'

'I was Vanstone's registrar.'

'Oh dear. Were you indeed?' How are the mighty fallen, Warr thought. This young man must have been marked out for success. 'Of course,' he added, 'Vanstone is extraordinarily able, there's no doubt about that. Very quick-witted. Apt to be a little intolerant, though.'

'He certainly is not prepared to tolerate me any longer,' Hugh said with some bitterness.

'You must find it a very difficult adaptation to have to make,' Warr said. 'You must miss the Central.'

'Yes.' Hugh paused. 'I tell myself I ought not to, but I'm afraid I do. Constantly.'

'I think it's only understandable. I expect you keep taking a backward look, and then wishing you hadn't eh?' He spoke with a sympathy that warmed Hugh, that made him want to unburden himself of his troubles.

'I do exactly that,' he agreed, with a sense of relief at being able to confide. 'It's – I know this, but I can't help it, all the same – it's a form of self-indulgence, all this glancing back. I don't like it, it isn't good for me, and it's a damn nuisance for everyone else, but I can't stop myself.'

'"*Nessun maggior dolore*",' Warr quoted in a gentle voice. 'You know that? From the *Inferno*.

'*Nessun maggior delore,*
Che ricordarsi del tempo felice
Nella miseria.

"No greater sorrow than to recall days of happiness in times of misery", roughly speaking. It's very true. One should really break oneself of the habit of the backward look – it helps no one.'

Hugh saw Jock Calderwood's eyes go to Warr, in pity and understanding, and knew that there must be some tragedy here. Colin Warr had been through a purgatory of his own, and Calderwood evidently knew it. The effect of this was to lessen, immediately, the drama that was seething in him at the exposure of his own past. After all, he reminded himself, others have pasts too, though they don't necessarily brandish them unsuitably over glasses of sherry before dinner. He made a brisk return to urbanity. 'Ideally,' he said, 'one should live in the present moment – and what could be more pleasant?' he added politely to his host.

Typical Ravelston superficiality, Calderwood thought, irritated. Just as Warr was ready to help him.

Hugh had somewhat the same reaction. He despised this smooth self who had suddenly appeared as much as the uncouth oaf who had been there a minute earlier. It seemed that he didn't care overmuch for either side of his personality. He forced himself back into a sincere response. Better to be uncouth than phony. He picked up the conversation where he had left it and gave it a shove in a different direction. 'After all, there's nothing here and now for agony,' he added quickly, 'and this is reality. Here and now. Not the past. Why not try living in it, I ask myself? Easier for me – and easier for everyone else too, I should imagine.' He gave Calderwood a disarmingly wry smile, that recognised something of what the older man had had to put up with during the past months from his difficult new research assistant. 'Better not look back, as you say.'

'So what do you do?' Warr asked. 'Bloody well look back in anger – or sorrow – isn't that so? One can't help it. Others have been there before, and know all about it, know what a mistake all the agonising can be. But each of us has to live his own misery.'

Hugh was committed now to self-revelation. 'Yes,' he admitted. 'It brings me nothing but discomfort and dissatisfaction, it gets me nowhere, but I go on doing it, I waste time in regret and self-accusation and dreams of how it would be, if only...'

'Wearing yourself out,' Warr said gently. He smiled with a sweetness that transformed his blunt features.

'The trouble is that it wears other people out, not just me,' Hugh said regretfully.

'Oh, I can put up with you a bit longer, if you mean me,' Calderwood said, knowing that he did, and that he had just been offered a back-handed apology for the months during which Hugh Ravelston had sat in his laboratory like an angry dark cloud. An angry dark cloud of which at times he had been very tired, so that he had often regretted his decision to take Hugh on. At this moment he forgave him all this.

They went into dinner. Honesty had forced itself into the conversation – as it was apt to do when Colin Warr was present. He had no time to waste on pretentious mouthings or conventional exchanges, but went to the root of the matter. The evening was a success, though after this they left Hugh's past alone. But a day or two later Warr asked Hugh to have a drink with him in the Dog and Duck. His compassion had been aroused, and during the weeks that followed Hugh spent several evenings talking to him, out at his cottage. This was an attractive old place, built of the local flint. It was small, with one big living-room downstairs, with white-painted bookcases round the walls, a big open fire, comfortable chairs, one or two pleasant pieces of mellowed old oak, and a great piano.

Judith Warr, who was twenty years younger than her husband, was a pianist. Before her marriage she had lived in London, where she had concert engagements and played with a quartet that was slowly making a name. In addition she taught. The piano had been Colin's wedding present to her. She already had a piano, of course, and this remained in the London flat. She went up there twice a week. At the cottage she practised for a phenomenal number of hours daily, and in addition taught at the Brookhampton Grammar School two mornings a week. She had a busy life, but seldom showed this, for she was a tranquil girl, and well organized. She had large brown eyes flecked with what Colin called marmalade lights. Her hair too was the colour of marmalade, and thick, usually gathered into a loose knot at the nape of her neck, though sometimes hanging loosely beside her wide cheeks.

Although she seemed calm and tranquil, and provided Colin and Hugh, on the evenings he spent at the cottage, with huge meals apparently effortlessly, she became a different creature when she played. Hugh was amazed the first time he saw this happen. She sat down at her piano and played Bach to them – all very gracious. But it wasn't. Suddenly she was as one possessed. Some inner fire, hitherto not glimpsed by Hugh, shone out, and she played with a controlled intensity that staggered him, and showed her as a much more forceful personality than he had imagined.

He soon found that he valued the friendship of both the Warrs, that their companionship had changed his existence at Brookhampton. He took them for a day's sailing, on a calm, clear September day, with barely enough wind to keep them on the move, the estuary calm and untroubled. On another day Hugh and Colin had a picnic lunch on board *Sea Goose*. This was on a fine warm Saturday in early October, when Judith was in London until the evening.

They had finished lunch, *Sea Goose* was lying swinging on her moorings at the turn of the tide. They were drinking mugs of coffee in the cockpit and talking about Hugh's future. 'Of course,' Warr said suddenly, 'I expect you've changed a good deal in the last year. I expect you want different things from life now, eh? Presumably you were rather a different character as Vanstone's registrar? Or am I wrong?' He smiled quizzically at Hugh.

Now it all poured out. 'You are not wrong,' Hugh assured him. 'I was a very brash young man. So it seems.' How long ago had this become clear to him? He couldn't say, but he was thankful to admit it, to tell Warr what he had learnt about himself. 'For instance, I despised, I'm ashamed to say, people who were swayed by their private troubles in working hours. Now, of course, I've discovered that my own emotions can play merry hell with my work. This came as a tremendous surprise to me, you know. But there's no getting away from it. I still drift through the day in a haze of nostalgia. It makes me slow as a wet week sometimes. I make resolutions. Never again. Put your head down, Ravelston, and work. And then I catch myself dreaming again, and wonder how long I've wasted this time. Because I've no idea.' He stared out to sea, past *Sea Goose*'s mast, frowning and tense.

'You know,' Warr said comfortably, 'this is merely the process of adaptation. You'll come through. No good trying to hurry it.'

'About time I did. I'm just a nuisance to myself and everyone else.'

Warr chuckled. 'Oh proud Ravelston,' he said softly, his mouth gentle with kindly amusement. 'You'll have to put up with the fact that you're a nuisance to others. Most of us are from time to time. We're all dependant on one another. You're not the great exception.'

Hugh frowned. He didn't like it.

'Hard to take?' Warr asked. 'Just life, my boy. And you've learnt one quite valuable lesson *en route*. You've discovered at first hand that not only are we not in control of our destinies, but hardly even of ourselves. The beginning – however unwelcome – of humility. You'll be far more use to your patients, as a result.'

Hugh opened his mouth and shut it again on an unuttered protest. Enough of his lamentations.

However, Warr read his expression quite easily. 'One day you'll have patients to look after again,' he said firmly. 'And I can tell you from personal experience that it's perfectly possible to lead a valuable – and enjoyable – life even when diverted from the main road one confidently saw stretching ahead in one's salad days, straight to the goal. There's a lot to be said, too, for a career away from one's teaching hospital. Away from the rat race. Less exciting perhaps, but less neurotic, too. More genuine, often. The job for its own sake. Not for the purpose of achieving the next tiny step on the all-important ladder.'

This was it.

'What happened to you, then?' Hugh asked.

Warr sighed. 'Simply tragedy,' he said. 'It comes to a surprising number of people in a lifetime, and it came to me. I was married. I loved my wife – this is rarer than you might think – and we had a small daughter. She was a poppet, my Libby.' He smiled reminiscently, no pain in his smile, but happy remembrance. 'We were expecting another child, and Alison was visiting her mother – I was still in London, I was busy. I was after a consultant post at my own hospital, at that time. Alison had the car, and she was driving down from Scotland, and had a crash. They were both killed. That was that. No more family.'

Hugh exclaimed in sadness, and hit his fist on the boom. 'How does one take something like that?' he asked. 'Here am I, with my potty little career gone phut, acting up all over the place, impossible to live with. But this – this was big, real, inescapable. Not just lost hopes, but living relationships broken–'

'I didn't think you knew much about those,' Colin said proddingly. This was a half-truth.

'Not much,' Hugh agreed. 'I used to think I did, but I don't. My girl-friend – not Angela Carlton, the one I'd dropped Angela for, which was probably the cause of the trouble – well, in her turn she dropped me, once I wasn't the coming young man. Serve me right. But I was very stunned by it. She's marrying my cousin. I find this very hard to take.'

'I should think so, too,' Warr agreed. He had known nothing about Nicola.

'I thought we had something that mattered, you see. That there was something real between us. I was going to marry Nicky. If our relationship had gone wrong, you know, I think I could have understood it, seen my own part in it. But this negation of all meaning between us, this cancellation of something I had thought was alive and genuine – the best thing in my life, I'd imagined.' He shrugged. 'Imagined is the word. It can't have been there at all, the relationship I'd thought we'd shared. However–' his eyes came back from the distance, focused on Warr. 'It's nothing compared with your loss.

But, as I say, I find it very difficult to manage. So how did you manage?'

'Oh, I didn't,' Warr said. 'I handled it just about as badly as I could have. I had nothing to do with any of my friends, I gave them the cold shoulder – and God knows they tried, some of them – I was impossible to deal with, and, as you say, I couldn't work. My loss came between me and work, all the time. I couldn't get away from it. I was hell all round. I didn't get the consultant post I'd been after. I don't honestly see how they could have given it to me, in the frame of mind I was in. Anyway, there were plenty of others after it, I wasn't the most outstanding by any means, it would have been touch and go in any case, even if I'd been at my best, instead of my worst.'

'So then what?'

'So I hung around disagreeably for a year or two, and then began to put in for jobs outside London. At one time I wouldn't have touched them. Eventually I landed up here. A good deal later I met Judith. The rest you know – or most of it.'

Something stopped Hugh from saying 'and now you've come through, you've built a new life, you've got Judith,' or any words of that sort. An instinct, perhaps, that all was not well, some diagnostic flair that had often helped him in the wards at the Central. He said nothing, and after a moment, turned and looked at Warr, questioningly. He saw the heavy burly figure, in an open-necked shirt and knitted sweater today, the thick neck, the kindly plain face, a little weary, but relaxed, peaceful. No torment, but some sadness. That was only to be expected, given that history. The warning came again. There was something else. Something wrong.

'There's something else,' he stated. 'Isn't there?'

'You're very acute,' Warr said. 'I see why Vanstone had you. Yes, there's something else.' He brooded, saying nothing, sitting slouched in the cockpit, heavy, limp. Knowledge swept through Hugh, and he wondered how he had missed it over these months. Of course, the reason might in part have been that he was used to Colin's appearance in dark formal suits, with stiff collar and tie. He had not seen him often in the loose-fitting sweater he was wearing today.

Warr looked at him. 'Well, what is it?' he snapped at him, as if they were on a teaching round.

Hugh wouldn't say. He might be wrong. He hoped he was – his assessment was little more than an intuition. In any case, he couldn't be certain, if he was right, that Warr knew. He dared not risk an answer.

'Well?' War asked again. 'Surely,' he jibed, 'you can make a diagnosis when it's staring you in the face?'

Hugh wouldn't, and Warr made it for him. 'I've got Hodgkin's,' he said.

'I suppose you're quite sure?' Hugh asked.

'Quite. Anyway, you'd seen it for yourself. I watched you see it.' He fingered his neck thoughtfully.

'Of all the bloody luck,' Hugh said, and swore. 'How–' he began. 'I mean, when–'

'A couple of years ago. I reckon I've got another two or three years, if I'm lucky.'

There was no answer to this. This was probably all he had. There was no cure. This was what Calderwood had known, when he looked so sad that evening. Colin Warr was dying, and knew it.

VI

One evening, Colin Warr and Hugh were having a drink in the back room of the Dog and Duck, opposite the hospital, at the end of the day. Warr began talking about a child he had just seen with a congenital heart lesion.

'Not much one can do for her, I'm afraid,' Warr said. 'And personally, I don't think the surgeons will want her yet, though I've referred her to Boardman.' He discussed the possible lines of treatment for a while, because he could see that Hugh was enjoying the talk, and he realised how much he must miss the medical discussions he was used to at the Central. Typically, he followed the realisation by plunging into the heart of the matter.

'What do you miss most, now you've left the hurly burly behind you for the quiet of the laboratory?' he asked.

'Well,' Hugh hesitated. 'Just that, I suppose. The hurly burly. Being in the thick of things. I must be one of those people who thrive on being in the centre of the storm. I'm not cut out, I don't think, for a contemplative life, or a quiet laboratory routine. It's probably very good for me,' he added quickly. He didn't want to give the impression that this was another complaint. 'Time I took a long hard look at myself.'

'I daresay,' Warr agreed. 'We all have to come to it sometime, and it does no harm, once or twice in a lifetime. A good stare inside can be most...' he searched for a word.

'Salutary,' Hugh supplied. 'Though a little depressing.'

'Don't you like what you see?' Warr asked at once.

'No, not much.'

'Is this – er – somewhat of a surprise to you?'

Hugh grinned, and raised his eyebrows in

self-mockery. 'I'm afraid so,' he admitted. 'I realise now that I was rather pleased with me, a year ago.' He hunched his shoulders.

'You are probably beginning to grow up,' Colin suggested.

'And about time too.'

'But always a difficult process. And often tiresome for the onlooker also.' Warr, as usual, did not pull his punches, and Hugh winced visibly. 'How old are you, anyway?'

'Twenty-six.'

'I should say you're having to do your growing up rather all at once and not under ideal conditions. However, you'll have to learn to accept yourself as you are some-time. The real you, not the idealised figure you used to kid yourself you were. One day you'll suddenly comprehend that this is how everyone is, you're no worse than the others, if no better either. They are all little men trying to do their best, and you are one of them.' He shot a sudden look across the table. He didn't expect this to be taken well.

From the rueful glance Hugh returned he knew his judgement was correct.

'I can't quite see myself in that role,' Hugh began, and broke off. 'At least, that's not true. It's exactly how I see myself, with a dull shock and a sense of depression, for brief periods. A little man like everyone else. But I don't like it, and I gradually begin to feel better, until next time. I decide I'm not such a bad chap after all.'

'And not a little man?' Warr asked, grinning. 'You didn't take to that, did you?'

'No.'

'No one does. But once you accept it, in some ways the knowledge is comforting. In any case, a glimpse of our own littleness from time to time is most humanising. These glimpses, coupled with a sense of proportion, are of considerable assistance when we can't have our own little way all the bloody time.'

'And why should anyone expect that?' Hugh asked, suddenly passionate. 'Look at that child you've just been talking about. There are hundreds of them, handicapped in one way or another, here in Brookhampton alone. That child will be damn lucky if she lives to do her eleven plus. And if she does she'll go to a secondary modern school housed in an old Victorian building in a back street. She'll be in the C stream, because apart from not being very bright anyway, she'll have missed half her schooling coming in and out of hospital. If she reaches adult life, she'll do a routine job for a few years, then marry some labourer and start bringing up kids before she's had a chance to see what life can hold for some who are luckier than she is. In any case, she'll probably never get that far. She'll more likely see only her primary school and the back street where she lives – one of those back streets that occasionally cause me to indulge in bouts of ridiculous self-pity, simply because I'm living – perfectly comfortably, mind you – in one for a few years. I can't wait to get out. Dreary. Noisy. She'll never know anywhere else. All her life, too, she'll be tired and below par, not up to her dull little friends even, everything an effort. Then her brief life will inevitably end – and what's she had out of it?' He spread his hands helplessly. That gesture, and the little case-history, all too typical, as Colin knew, told him something about Hugh Ravelston that he had wanted to know. He decided then to use Hugh on the research project – on Sodium Metabolism and Body Fluids in Hypertension – which he had begun some years earlier, and for which Jock Calderwood, who was the great organiser at the Brookhampton General, had just managed to obtain a grant for clerical and technical assistance.

'I'll use Ravelston on it – you've about finished with him, haven't you?'

'Good. I hoped you might.'

'Oh, I saw the wheels going round all right, the first evening I met him.'

'I wanted you to make up your own mind without prejudice.'

'That's what I've been doing. I like him.'

'I'm beginning to like him,' Calderwood agreed. 'I used not to. He's Ben's friend, you know. They were at Garside together, then Clare, then the Central.'

'I didn't realise they knew one another as well as that, though I assumed they'd met at the Central. I imagine Ben got him here?'

'Well, yes and no. He badgered me about it. I wasn't keen on the idea. But Ben and Hugh have been thick as thieves ever since they were in the Upper Fourth. I must admit I used to wish Ben had chosen anyone else as a friend. I know the Ravelstons, and I've never cared for them. No heart, all brain, the lot of them. Supercilious, too, and moneyed. However, Ben's always stuck up for Hugh, and I've often wondered if there was more in him than met the eye, because my son's not indiscriminate about people, as a rule. But, as I say, I didn't want to have Hugh here when he was struck off. Well, would you? Ben begged me to, of course. I don't think I would have given in, though, if Ramsay hadn't rung me up himself and asked me to. You know Ramsay?'

'Alec Ramsay, yes, I know him vaguely. Nice chap, I've always heard.'

'He said he had a soft spot for Hugh Ravelston, seemed to think he'd been done a certain amount of dirt. Anyway, I took him, and I must say, I often wished I hadn't. He went through a very bad patch when he arrived, and I got thoroughly tired of him. Moody, silent, lowering, wouldn't speak, did hardly any work. If it hadn't been that he was unmistakably suffering, I would have given him hell. As it was, I hadn't even the satisfaction of being able to let off steam that way. In spite of myself, though, I became fond of him. Don't quite know why. I'm glad you'll use him. You realise, of course, that he'll almost certainly not get back on the register when his case comes up again – next month, I think.'

Warr sighed. 'Yes, I'd taken that into account. I only hope he has, poor devil.'

'Doubt it. Don't see how one could. However, as far as you're concerned, I'd say you're probably getting a bargain, at cut price. He's over the worst now. He'll work better for you than he ever did for me, blast him.'

'I hope so,' Colin agreed. 'I plan to have him more or less running the project. He's perfectly capable of it, as you say. I'd never get anyone of his background, in the ordinary way.'

'Well, you'd better tell him what you've planned for him.'

'Unless you'd rather. He's on your staff at present.'

'He'll have to talk to you about the project, so you might as well break the news, too. You can say we've discussed it. I'll give you accommodation – that'll be my contribution.'

'Apart from the inestimable benefit of your pathological guidance.'

'My pathological guidance is a very old stale joke, and I'm getting rather tired of hearing it. You all seem to imagine it's your own personal discovery.'

'Sorry. My sense of humour is a bit prep school, Judith tells me.'

'Oh, I wouldn't say that, Col. First year medical school.'

'Thanks.'

'Colin, have you seen Taylor lately?'

Taylor was the senior consultant in general medicine at Brookhampton.

'Not for a month or two,' Warr said, frowning.'

'I think you should, you know. You're tiring too easily. Doing too much, if you ask me. Any fever?'

'No, blast you. What an encouraging chap you are, Jock.'

'No good being an ostrich, old boy. We can look after you all right if you'll only co-operate a little. You'll make old bones yet.'

'Oh no, I shan't. Don't let's delude ourselves.'

'You will if you're sensible.'

Colin gave Jock Calderwood a thoughtful look, which he had no difficulty in interpreting. 'Don't look at me as if I'm not up to hearing the brutal truth,' he said.

'Well, who do you think you're kidding?'

'Neither you nor myself. I know it's dicey, all of us know it's dicey, no one's attempting to deny that. But people have come through before. No reason why you shouldn't.'

'One in a hundred, perhaps. The cases I've seen have had two to five years from diagnosis. Anyway, I don't want to be pulled through with careful management for an extra eighteen months. All I want is to live a normal life for as long as I can. I don't want to be any sort of sample try-out for new remedies and treatments that might prolong my existence for a few hard-won months, at the cost of feeling physically ill and spiritually agonised for twice that time, only to make a splendid subject for a clinico-pathological conference after my unfortunate decease before I'd had time to respond to the latest treatment by Blaxo's newest methyl-hydrazine derivative. And I don't want Judith to be in torment for months.'

Calderwood sighed. Colin had thought it all out to the end. There were some at the hospital who considered he was hardly aware of his diagnosis, the knowledge, they asserted, sat so lightly on his shoulders. Calderwood had always known they were wrong, but now he saw just how wrong. Colin Warr had lived through a nightmare in his imagination. The tragedy was that the nightmare would one day become reality, and he knew this.

'See Taylor, there's a good chap,' was all he said.

'Perhaps. I'll see Ravelston first, though. I want to get this project moving. When can he start?'

'Well, we're over the holiday period now. I've been getting him to help out generally. My paper on auto-immune antibody response is in the press. I'd like to have him to check the proofs with me later, but apart from that I should say you can have him next week, if you like.'

'I would like. There are all my scrappy jottings, and case-notes for five years to be collated. There are piles of ECGs to be cut up. There's a month's work, before we even begin. Then when we start the tests, we want up-to-date blood pressures and cardiographs. I'll do those, and he can do sedimentation rates and serum potassiums, and look after the paperwork. I suppose we shall have to buy some apparatus. Ravelston can work that out with you, eh? He'll get far more out of you than I would. He must know by now what you've got in that vast depository of yours – that is, if anyone knows, which I sometimes doubt.'

'If you knew how short of apparatus we are, and how we're reduced to using obsolete, outworn–'

'Stuff.'

They glared at one another.

'In the old days–' Calderwood began, and then stopped. 'Oh, never mind,' he said.

'What's the good? You have a talk to young Hugh, and I'll find a corner for you to keep your bits and pieces.'

Hugh would never forget that first talk with Colin Warr about his research project. It was the light at the end of the tunnel, the harbinger of a working life that might again have purpose. Warr had been almost apologetic when he described Hugh's proposed duties as his research assistant.

'There will be an immense amount of dreary routine,' he warned him. 'A mass of statistical checking, repeated recording of results, and so on.'

'I can take it,' Hugh replied with a grin.

'As long as you know what you're in for.'

'As long as *you* know what *you're* in for,' Hugh pointed out, his face changing. This was difficult, but he must say it, in fairness to Warr. 'You know that my case comes up to the Disciplinary Committee next month? I haven't a more than fifty-fifty chance of finding myself back on the register.'

'Nasty to have that hanging over you,' Warr said. 'Doesn't matter to me, though. Your bad luck is my good fortune. I propose to make use of you – dammit, what are you worrying about? If you were on the register I shouldn't have the remotest chance of nabbing you for a dogsbody – and a dogsbody is what you'll be, don't imagine you won't. I can be a demanding so-and-so.'

'I'm quite prepared for demands to be made. Grateful for the opportunity.'

'Nothing to be grateful for,' Warr said brusquely.

'Oh, yes, I have.' Hugh was certain about this, and he was determined to make it clear. 'You're giving me a chance and I'm damn lucky to have it. Don't think I don't recognise it.'

'I don't think you'll let me down,' Warr said seriously. 'In any case, I'm investing in you. I'm hoping that later on you'll play a larger part in the project, when we've got it under way, and I can step back and take my own ease. That's why I count myself lucky to have you, and not some new biochemical graduate.' This was only partly true. He said it because he thought Hugh Ravelston needed encouragement, and because he wanted to make it clear that he expected him to stick to the assignment. Hugh Ravelston, Warr knew, undoubtedly had a first-class mind, and from that point of view what he had just said was correct. He was lucky to have him. But he was taking a chance. Why had they been so hard on him at the Central? They were not given to throwing out good men. Yet he had been told that even if Ravelston had not been off the register – which had undoubtedly been a shock to everyone – he would not have obtained another post at his teaching hospital. Why was this? Surely not simply because Vanstone had turned against him? Or was it? Such events had been known in the past. Or because his powerful grandfather had been old and crotchety, and had wanted a young fool taught a hard lesson? In the laboratory at Brookhampton, Warr had found out, Hugh Ravelston had the reputation of possessing a difficult temperament. Calderwood, who was not noted for seeking excuses for Hugh, discounted this, saying it was a passing phase in the process of adjustment. Warr himself thought this likely. Well, he would see. He would take him on, and find out his strengths and his weaknesses.

So Hugh's life began again to move. The worst, it seemed, was behind him. He supposed that the intervening period had served its purpose. He was not used, as he had said, either to a routine job or to solitude. Both had been hard to take. But in that solitary year, he had seen not only the popular Hugh Ravelston of the past, with the world before him, but the secret Hugh Ravelston. He had tried to come to grips with both of them. He had gone looking, for the first time, for himself. Now he looked outward again.

One of the first people he saw was Sandra Clifford. Sandra was the Cliffords' only child, and at this time she was ten. She was always in and out of hospital, always ailing. Pasty-faced and chesty, she looked a typical undernourished city child, and was a constant embarrassment to Mrs Clifford, who was a perfectionist.

'That child ought to see a doctor.'

'Doesn't get enough to eat – it stands to reason. What she needs is a few square meals. That Irene Clifford. Goes out to work, always buying new clothes. If she stayed in and did some good home-cooking, it'd be more to the point.'

'Never takes her out, neither. Sandra could do with a bit of fresh air, that's what I say. Why don't her mother take her for a nice blow out by the marshes, go for a picnic, instead of letting her stay cooped up all day in the house with the telly? That never did no good to anybody. Not surprising she's off her food, if you ask me.'

But there was far more to it than this, as Hugh could see once he considered the question. Sandra was not simply a peaky child, spoilt and picking up infection when she went to school. She was doomed, not to any dramatic illness, but to the steady attrition of a chronic condition for which there existed no cure, a condition which left her thoroughly unattractive in person and character. She seldom felt well, she snuffled and choked, her food did her little good, she was bored with her dreary existence and whined, she was irritable and petty. She had missed so much schooling that sometimes she appeared almost mentally deficient. She was afraid of the outside world, knowing that she cut a poor figure, afraid of life. Afraid, too, of her mother. Somewhere inside her dwarfed personality she knew she was a bitter disappointment, that her mother could hardly forgive her for being the child she was.

Irene Clifford was a pretty, tense creature, with dark hair always well cared for, a slight youthful figure, who dressed attractively. She radiated energy, cleanliness and drive. If she had had six children she would have had initiative and ambition enough to make a way in the world for all of them. But she had only Sandra, and she was bitterly ashamed of her. She had seen herself as the perfect mother, bringing up charming children, supplying love and food and the good life to a thriving family, the admiration of the neighbourhood.

Irene Clifford was eaten alive by ambition and the desire to shine – in Malden Road, in Mrs Calderwood's house (she was Mrs Calderwood's daily woman), in the church, before the tradespeople. She appreciated working for Mrs Calderwood, and was always willing to put in extra time at weekends, if there were guests staying in the house, or in the evening, if they had a dinner party. These were the people she would have liked to live among, the people whom, in her dreams, her children would have joined. She was, in short, a terrific snob, and could be overthrown completely if referred to as Mrs Calderwood's daily woman, rather than as her help. Sometimes she alluded to herself as Mrs Calderwood's housekeeper. Mrs Calderwood, under the impression that she did her own housekeeping quite adequately, would have had a shock.

When Hugh had come as a lodger, Mrs Clifford had been delighted. One step nearer the Calderwoods' world. She had been greatly disappointed when, in answer to her enquiry, Hugh had told her – rather bluntly and disagreeably, she considered – that he was not a doctor. She had looked forward to calling him doctor. Having a doctor living in her house would have increased her status in the neighbourhood, and she had imagined herself saying to callers 'Yes, the doctor's in, I'll tell him you're here,' or 'no, I'm afraid the doctor had to go out, but he asked me to tell you…' 'The doctor likes his food just so,' she could have told the neighbours, or 'as I said to the doctor only yesterday.' Her opinion of Hugh went down. She asked him what he did, and he told her he worked in Dr Calderwood's laboratory at the hospital. 'On research, perhaps?' she had asked avidly. He mumbled vaguely, but Irene Clifford had already made up her mind. 'He's a research worker,' she told them in Malden Road. 'Very important research up at the hospital.' Anyone in Irene Clifford's environment had to reflect credit on her.

This was where Sandra let her down. She would not admit it to herself, but she hated the child. From the time she had brought her home from the hospital as a baby, she had found her revolting. Obsessionally clean and tidy herself, she had found the care of her baby degrading. The house smelt of Sandra's nappies, and Irene Clifford loathed the tiny creature she had produced. She was saddled with an unattractive encumbrance, and often the hate she concealed from herself poured out of her mouth in the harsh and strident tones she used to her daughter, so unlike the soft appealing voice Mrs Calderwood heard from her.

If only something could be done about the girl. She didn't get any better. Surely there must be something they could *do* at the hospital? Heaven knew the child spent enough time there.

Mrs Clifford seldom mentioned Sandra to the Calderwoods, except to report that 'she wasn't too bad, considering' or 'she'd gone into hospital again' when Mrs Calderwood asked after her. The less said about Sandra the better. The child let her down.

But there was no hiding her from Hugh. He could hear her whining and grumbling, he heard Mrs Clifford's exasperation with her, he knew when she was in bed again. He heard her coughing and spluttering. He would often ask about her – he seemed interested in her, for some reason. This irritated Mrs Clifford. She began to complain to him about Sandra. After all, he worked at the hospital, even if he wasn't a doctor. He must know *something*.

'Surely they could *do* something about her?' she demanded. 'She's been going up there all her life, and she doesn't get a bit better.'

Hugh sighed. If his supposition was correct, there was hardly any chance that she would. 'If there's anything they could do,' he assured her, 'I'm sure they would. But really, you know, no one can help her as much as you.'

This was what they all said. This wasn't what she went up to the hospital for, simply to be told that it was all up to her. She could have stayed at home for that. What were hospitals for? It was their job to do something about Sandra.

'I don't know why they don't keep her in,' she said in disgruntled tones. 'It's almost impossible for me to manage her. She needs proper nursing.'

'Have you told the doctor at the clinic so?'

As a matter of fact she hadn't. She was always meaning to, always rehearsing what she'd say when she saw him, but when she was confronted by the paediatrician in his white coat, in the busy outpatient department where she saw him each month, she was overawed. He looked kindly at her and said 'Really, it's all up to you, Mrs Clifford. I know it's hard for you, but her future is in your hands.'

Not only did Irene Cifford hardly dare to do anything but agree with whatever he said. She also longed to stand well with him, to impress him with her devotion and her capability. She exerted all her charm – which was considerable – to win him over, and genuinely felt, as she faced him, that she would throw her whole personality into cherishing her daughter. Her sincerity was patent. Dr Harrington was convinced of her desire to help Sandra, and thought she was one of his most sensible mothers.

So did his registrar, Maxwell Okiya. 'Fortunately,' he said to Hugh, 'the mother's very good. It all depends on her, of course. There's practically nothing we can do.' He shrugged his shoulders, and spread his hands expressively. 'Well, you know,' he added. Hugh's story had now gone round among the resident medical staff, spread by Dr Moyall, Warr's registrar. There had been more interested glances as he went about the corridors, but he could stand those. On the whole he was glad they knew. The secrecy had been a mistake. People, of course, were not all that interested in him anyway, he told himself (he was wrong here), and he would have done better to have concealed nothing.

He had thought he might have had to explain himself to Dr Okiya. He had gone in search of him at the end of outpatients. Okiya greeted him warmly, his dark face mobile and friendly.

'Hullo,' he said. 'Aren't you Ravelston?'

'Yes,' Hugh said. 'I am. If you have a minute I wanted to ask you about a child who attends the clinic – I lodge with her parents.'

'Oh yes?'

'Sandra Clifford.'

'Sandra Clifford? We'd better have a look, hadn't we?' He asked for the case-notes, and peered at them when they were handed to him. 'M-hm. Yes. Sandra Clifford. Cystic fibrosis of the pancreas. Oh yes, I remember her.' Then he made the remark about Mrs Clifford being a good mother, the validity of which Hugh doubted, though he had enough tact to keep his mouth shut. No good trying to teach the paediatricians their own business. They knew their mums – or thought they did.

They discussed Sandra's case in some detail, however.

'Of course,' Okiya said, 'she picks up every infection that's going, and they take hell out of her.'

'The mother's a bit depressed, you know, because she feels that Sandra's not making any progress.'

'Of *course* she's not making any progress. It's all she can do not to slip back all the time. By running hard, she can just about manage to stay in the same place. But you know this as well as I do.'

'Now I know the diagnosis, yes. I suspected it before, but I hoped I might be wrong, of course. Such an event has been known to occur from time to time.'

'If you were Vanstone's registrar, I don't imagine it happened very often,' Okiya remarked. 'By Jove,' (Hugh was later to discover that Okiya was given to these old-fashioned ejaculations, adopted from the muscular Christian who had been his headmaster at the mission school where he had begun his education). 'By Jove, I would give my soul to have had a chance like that.'

Hugh experienced a deep sense of guilt. Okiya had the reputation of being a good sound physician. He had come a long way, from his African village to medical school at Ibadan, in Nigeria, then to the Institute of Child Health in London, and now to the Brookhampton General. There was no chance that he would ever be Vanstone's registrar, though. But if he had been, Hugh thought, he would have made a better job of it than he himself had done. To Hugh it had all been handed on a plate, all the opportunities that others scrambled and prayed for. He had taken everything for granted, had hardly valued it, and had gone uncaring through the days that others would have turned into profit. Okiya had fought every step of the way – it was not only Sandra Clifford, he thought, who had to run very hard in order to stay in the same place.

'You would have done better in it than I did,' he said with sincerity.

'Quite likely not,' Okiya said with a glint of humour. 'We Africans also are rather given to driving expensive cars too fast, you know. It's one of our failings – frequently getting us into trouble.'

You Africans are a very nice lot, Hugh thought. The sympathy and acceptance could not have been more tactfully offered. Okiya was now rummaging through a pile of X-rays, demanding an opinion.

The following week-end Hugh took him sailing. Okiya was frozen, and refused to accompany him a second time. However, this was the beginning of a friendship between them – and, of course, of a régime of treatment for Sandra Clifford that could hardly have been improved if she had been a millionaire's child. For all practical purposes she had two personal physicians. They brooded over her history, they tested her, they watched her every reaction, they X-rayed her, they changed her diet, they took her in, they sent her home. Short of taking her apart and putting her together again – which was what the poor child needed – they did everything that could be done. Hugh himself spent hours with the physiotherapists learning how to supervise her exercises. When she was at home he saw her night and morning, and the half-hour he spent with her making her drain her chest, making her cough – which made all the difference to her well-being, and which could have been done by Irene Clifford, except that she lacked the necessary patience for it – taught him to know her condition as he had never known any patient's before.

At this time his application to have his name restored to the register came before the General Medical Council. It was a year since they had ordered it to be erased. At times it seemed like ten years to him.

The Council refused to restore his name, and he was back where he had been a year earlier, plunged into introspection, recrimination and regret. He had told himself to hope for nothing, he had reminded himself that his life was interesting, far from empty, even that he was learning a great deal that he might have missed if he had remained at the Central.

He intended to tell no one what had happened. He went through his day's work with determined concentration, refusing to deviate from the E.S.R.s and serum potassiums from Warr's clinic. At least, he told himself, at least there'll be no more futile day dreams while the hours go by and the work piles up.

In the evening Colin Warr came up, to glance over the results. He took one look at Hugh, instead, and demanded 'What's the matter?'

'Is it written all over me?' Hugh asked. 'I was kidding myself I wasn't showing a thing. Poker-faced Ravelston, that's me, I thought.' He grinned, and added, 'The G.M.C. have turned me down again.'

'My dear chap, I am sorry. How bloody.' Warr sighed. 'Nothing to be done,' he said. 'It's like all these depressing hands that life deals out from time to time. Nothing to be done but live through it.'

'No doubt it's for my own good,' Hugh said ironically.

'That's up to you,' Warr said, taking his remark at its face value. 'What you make of it's in your hands. But one thing I have no doubt about. None at all. You must take the long view. This is only an interval, a brief interval in fact, in your life. Your medical career will be resumed, you know. If not this year, then next year. If not next year, then the year after. Don't lose heart. We all have our setbacks.' He sighed. 'How trite I sound. But then life is trite.'

'Hope deferred maketh the heart sick,'

Hugh amazed himself by saying. It summed up exactly what he felt, but he had not meant to come out with it, he had not meant to confide this to Warr, or anyone else.

'No one can get through life without suffering. One day you'll be able to look back, and remember.'

'Do you remember,' Hugh asked, going off at a tangent, 'you asked me once what I missed most, from my Central days? I said I missed being in the thick of things.'

'I remember.'

'That's not true any longer. I enjoy my life here now, there's no question about that. And there are compensations, after all, for not being in London. There's all the sailing, and being able to sleep on board *Sea Goose* and come in here in the morning, there's the fact that life isn't a long series of interruptions, with no opportunity for thought, and always working against time, always being tired – and getting, I'm sure, more and more stale. I needed a breather, and I've got it. In some ways I know this period has done me good. I needed pulling up short, I needed to disentangle myself from everything I used to imagine essential.' He paused.

'But?' Warr asked quietly.

'But.' Hugh repeated the word flatly. 'But. As you say. But I miss the patients. I never expected to. I miss clinical medicine, and I don't mean the use of my brain in diagnosis and treatment, I mean the contact with patients. I didn't know I was going to miss that. At first I didn't notice it, in all the other things I regretted. But that's what stays with me. That's what frustrates me, too. Dammit, I'm as good a doctor as half of them here, the clinics are over-crowded, the waiting lists run on for years. There's so much I could do, and I'm not bloody well allowed to.'

'I know you're being wasted,' Warr agreed. 'I said so, if you remember.'

'Yes. I know it's not important, in the general scheme. I know I have only myself to thank. And there are plenty of other things wrong, without me going on about the patients I think I could help. My frustration is a good deal my own selfishness, anyway. It's not so much the patients I could help, when it comes down to it, as the patients I miss. The effect they have on me, more than the effect I have on them. I miss dealing with people all the time.'

'It's a two-way traffic,' Warr agreed. 'Dealing with patients adds another dimension to daily life. In clinical medicine, you need more than intellectual ability. You have to have an instinct for human relationships to be any real use. This is what the working day should consist of – the skill of the brain and the heart together.'

'It's the relationships I miss – life seems

thin and arid without them.'

'Yes, I can understand that. You know, a lot of people accuse us of being crude and materialistic. Dealing with bodies – blood and bones – and riding roughshod over finer susceptibilities. One has to admit there's something in it. Compared with the fastidious, who go through existence touching others glancingly, delicately, where there is a true affinity – compared with them, we are coarse-fibred and obvious. I don't know which of us gets more out of life, but I can hazard a fairly good guess as to which of us gives more. But by ordinary conventional standards we are embarrassingly frank, obscene perhaps, in our conversation. That isn't approved of.'

Hugh grinned to himself. Margaret Calderwood had told him that Colin Warr was known for having disrupted many a dinner table. There were hostesses around Brookhampton who were afraid to invite him – 'my dear, he's such a pet, but one never knows what he's going to *say*. He may come out with *anything*.'

'You needn't sit there grinning. I know I'm said to go too far in that direction. I'm not one of these smooth types like your friend Vanstone with expensive private practices. But in medicine the unspeakable, barely thinkable has to be spoken and thought. Spiritual and physical are fused. Or should be. When they aren't, it's the spiritual that loses out. That's our big failing, I admit. Both can be fundamentally crude and unpleasing. There are facts we take for granted that would devastate anyone outside medicine. Emotional and physical tragedies. You never get used to this, but you learn to deal with it. You have to be ready to bring spiritual comfort to a frightened soul and at the same moment physical comfort to a heaving body. We sometimes default on the first, but almost never on the second. Sometimes we fail to deliver the comfort, and the lay public say it's a scandal, we're all as hard as nails.' He shrugged. 'They should try it themselves, and see how they make out.' He looked across at Hugh. 'I wish you could come back to it. It's the only life for people like us. That you can't is a shocking waste of time. Try not to look on it as more than that. Don't allow yourself to be despondent.'

'A good deal was missing from my life a year or two ago that I take for granted now,' Hugh said slowly, unwillingly. 'I shouldn't complain.'

'Oh, I think you're entitled to complain,' Warr said lightly. 'But try not to let it get you down.'

Hugh looked at him as he sat there, and wondered how much his own diagnosis got him down. He had perhaps two years of life ahead. He had already had one course of radiotherapy.

Life dealt some dirty tricks, Hugh thought. The particular dirty trick it had dealt him was minor compared with Warr's fate.

'Better get on,' he remarked. 'This is today's lot.'

He pushed a series of results at Warr, who began looking through them.

VII

That autumn, Sir Donald Ravelston died. He was eighty-five, and he had the death he would have chosen. He had a heart attack while happily polishing the brass on *Moon Maid*, and died without regaining consciousness, the same evening.

Hugh had not seen him since the day he had travelled down to East Callant to be interrogated about the car crash, though he had written several times to the old man – each letter, unfortunately, conveying further unwelcome information. His grandfather had never acknowledged his letters, he had had no dealings with Hugh after their final interview. Now it was too late. He could never win his grandfather's approval now.

He stopped, startled, and examined this

thought. Win his approval, indeed? What sort of childish reaction was this? If he was looking round still for approval, he thought, he was doomed to disappointment.

He went down to the funeral, at East Callant. The cottage again gave him the same strange sense of being half in his childhood, half in some other unknown life. *Moon Maid* lay on her moorings. Archie said they would sail her still, though he supposed they might as well sell the cottage. Or perhaps they should let the Penmans live there. Unless they agreed to move to Cambridge, of course. Jean could do with their help, in the house and garden. At present she had only a series of daily women. If the Penmans agreed to come to Cambridge, Archie said, it would certainly be best to sell Harbour Cottage. An end to childhood, Hugh thought – and why not?

None of them stayed after the funeral. Archie and Jean drove back to Cambridge, after what appeared to have been a satisfactory talk with the Penmans, and Don to London. Hugh went by train. To his relief, Don had not offered him a lift.

A few weeks later there was a memorial service, a vast and somewhat imposing occasion at All Souls, Langham Place. Archie read the lesson, and Sir Alexander Ramsay gave the address.

Hugh arrived a little late. The train had

been held up near Basingstoke, and again for ten minutes outside Waterloo. He managed to grab a taxi at once, but they were singing the first hymn as he went up the aisle and joined the family in the front pew. Across the way, as he stood nearest to the aisle, were Sir Alexander Ramsay and all the top brass from the Central, singing away lustily and looking at him out of the corners of their eyes.

Be blowed to the lot of them, he thought. He had come to pay his respects to the old man. They could speculate about him if they were interested.

Eighty-five years Donald Ravelston had lived. A long span of days. For over half a century he had worked in the wards and clinics of the Central. Medicine had changed in his fifty years of practice. When he had first been a consultant, for instance, there had been no insulin. Diabetes had meant death to thousands of children, a pathetic death from hunger and thirst in the middle of plenty. For most of his days, there had been no antibiotics. Tuberculosis had been a killer. Pneumonia carried off thousands each winter. He had seen the coming of penicillin, and had treated some of the first cases in the world in his wards at the Central.

What could it have mattered to him, what did it count in the scheme of his life, that he had failed to make something out of one of his grandsons? This was a loss to the grandson concerned, but it could have been nothing of the sort to the eminent physician, who had probably hardly noticed Hugh's disaster, except in so far as it damaged his profession. He had cared very little, one way or the other, whether Hugh came or went. For medicine he cared deeply.

He had had a distinguished career – which could be clearly seen from the numbers gathered to remember him. He had brought relief to many. He had treated thousands in his lifetime, and many families had been grateful to him, devoted, had thought of him as a god, a saviour. He had believed in medicine, he had taught generations of students not only the science of their calling, but also glimpses of the way of life in which he believed. 'To cure sometimes, to alleviate often, to comfort always,' he had quoted.

No wonder, Hugh thought, that I was a bitter disappointment to him. Now he will never know that I am not as uncaring as he imagined, that however foolishly I may behave, there is something of his spirit in me. I understand what he believed in, I share his belief, even if my execution is shaky.

The United Hospitals Choir sang *Abide with Me*, and Hugh found his eyes wet with tears for the old man, who had stood rocklike through his childhood and youth, passed now and irretrievable, and whom he

156

had loved.

After the service there was a great shaking of hands outside the church, and many invitations to lunch, all – typically – parried by Archie, who was in a hurry to return to Cambridge to continue some work that was engrossing him. 'No, no, many thanks indeed, but I've booked a table at the R.S.M. – just for the family,' he added pointedly. 'I have to drive back to Cambridge this afternoon. Just a quick bite, you know, and we're off – isn't that so, my dear?' Jean, who had evidently been rehearsed, backed him up firmly. 'Come along, Hugh,' Archie added. 'Where's Don? Oh, there you are. Better make a move, or we'll be here all afternoon.' He set off briskly, only to have his hand shaken yet again. Hugh paused behind him, and found Don doing the same. They looked at one another. He and Don seldom had anything to say, except when they quarrelled. Hugh hardly supposed Don expected congratulations on his engagement.

'There you are, m'boy. I saw you earlier, then I lost you.' Sir Alexander Ramsay materialised. He was, Hugh noted with a shock, older and more careworn than when he had last seen him two years earlier in his room, at the Central. He seemed as genial as ever. 'Well now,' he said cheerfully, 'come along, and tell me how you're getting on at Brookhampton – Archie, you're all lunching at the R.S.M., I hear? I'll return this young-ster of yours to you there.'

They walked round Cavendish Square, joining what amounted to a crocodile of medical men – many from the Central, but a number too from hospitals and practices scattered over the country – converging on the Royal Society of Medicine for susten-ance. Many interested glances noticed the youngest Ravelston, as good-looking and sleek as ever, despite his year in the wilderness – some of them found this genuinely surprising, having an unspoken but firm conviction that a year at a provincial hospital would in some way remove the gloss and alter a man's tailoring – walking with the Professor of Medicine, deep in talk.

'He'll be back,' they said to one another. 'The privilege of being a Ravelston – it can surmount even a small matter of being struck off.'

'Outrageous. If he were some unknown, he'd be finished.'

'I'm not so sure he isn't. They didn't let him back at the last meeting.'

'Did he apply?'

'I'm told on good authority that he did.'

'Perhaps Ramsay's simply explaining to him that he hasn't a hope in hell.'

'Surely Uncle Archie can always find him a post?' someone who disliked all Ravel-stons on principle asked caustically.

This in effect was what Ramsay was talking about. 'There won't be any difficulty about a laboratory job,' he pointed out. 'Don't worry – you'll get back on the register. Next year or the year after. And with your ability and your family behind you, there's no reason why you shouldn't do well. But clinical medicine is a different kettle of fish. I'm afraid you must expect to be very much hampered there.'

'I'm afraid it's clinical medicine I want to get back to, sir,' Hugh said definitely. 'If I've learnt anything, I've learnt that.'

Ramsay sighed. 'I'm sorry to hear you say that,' he admitted. 'Why can't you settle down to physiology, like your cousins?' he demanded.

'It's not for me, sir. It's a sideline.'

'Don't be ridiculous. It's basic, as you very well know. Don't be an obstinate fellow. Most of your family are perfectly at home in the laboratory – much more so than in the wards. This is not the time to decide to strike out on a line of your own. I'm going to tell you frankly – it's to your interest to stick to the bench. You have the brain for it, and you can have a worthwhile career there. Don't let some tomfool notion that you're a clinician make you spend the next few years banging your head unrewardingly against a brick wall.'

'That's what I feel inclined to do,' Hugh

said. 'I can see it's asking for trouble, sir. But I must at least try. I can't spend the rest of my life in the laboratory. I'd rather spend it in general practice.' He was startled to hear himself say this, but not as startled as Ramsay.

'Oh, my dear boy,' he said distressfully. 'No need for that, surely. Oh dear, we must see what we can do. Yes, indeed. But I do beg of you, try to entertain the prospect of a career outside clinical medicine. Otherwise it's going to be so very difficult, you know. What about biochemistry, if you dislike physiology? I agree, only don't tell y'r Uncle Archie I said so, physiology is perhaps a little inhuman. But biochemistry, now. Opening up almost daily, isn't it, eh? Fascinating possibilities. Fascinating. If I had my time over again, I assure you I wouldn't at all mind…' he sketched a neat biochemical career for himself, by which time they had reached the R.S.M. The porter immediately pounced on Ramsay, waving a sheaf of telephone messages.

Hugh went down to wash, feeling extraordinarily depressed. As he came upstairs to the hall to look for Archie and Jean, he met Ben, who seized on him, looking worried.

'There you are. I saw you with Ramsay, so I didn't like to interrupt. Then I lost you. What about lunch? How about going out and scrounging something? I want to hear

160

what Ramsay said. Anyway, this place is packed to the eyebrows.'

'Archie's booked a table,' Hugh began doubtfully. At this point Archie himself appeared. 'Come along,' he said, ringing for the lift. 'Can't hang about all day. Where's Jean? Oh, there you are. Where's Don?'

'I don't know,' Hugh said vaguely. He had lost sight of him when Ramsay came up.

'Oh well, he'll turn up,' Archie said comfortably.

This he now did, looking self-satisfied and with Nicola in tow. Hugh felt as though he had been jabbed unkindly in the stomach, and was momentarily winded. Don gave him a look of triumph, and announced, 'Here's Nicola.'

'So I see,' Archie replied disagreeably. Absent-minded he might appear on occasion – though this was more a matter of deliberate policy, linked with self-protection – but he had never had the slightest difficulty in assessing a situation at a glance when he wished. He took this one in instantaneously, with all its implications.

Nicola took a hand – she after all had been fully prepared for the encounter – and made charming cooing noises at everyone in turn.

'Mrs Ravelston ... not too tired from the journey?' (Does the girl think I'm in my eighties, Jean wondered crossly?) 'Professor Ravelston... Hugh darling, lovely to see you again, such a long time... Ben, it's been simply *ages,* where *have* you been all this time?'

Hugh darling scowled like a five-year-old, while Ben replied in a grating voice that he was seldom heard to use, 'Yes, it has been a long time, hasn't it?' The words were innocuous, but the tone said as clearly as though he had enunciated it syllable by syllable 'but not long enough for me.'

Jean looked distressed. She was upset on Hugh's behalf and angry with Don. At the same time she was miserable because she could see no happiness in the affair for Don, who she knew had taken up Nicola to spite Hugh. Jean remembered Don's helpless jealousy as a child, when Rodney, his adored elder brother, had begun to turn all his attention to Hugh. Don had never forgiven Hugh for this. Just now he was clearly pleased with himself, and impervious to any disapproval. He said brightly, 'Nicky can stay for lunch with us, isn't it splendid?'

'No, it isn't,' Archie said flatly. He was not standing for this. 'I booked a table for four, and I told you so.'

Don looked pointedly at Hugh, who saw he had no option but to do what Don had counted on him doing, and retire gracefully. 'Nicky can have my place,' he said producing an unseeing smile in her direction. 'I ought to be off anyway, and I–'

Ben put his oar in. He had seen this confrontation coming, having glimpsed Don with Nicola in Cavendish Square. His intention had been to manoeuvre Hugh away before their arrival. 'I want to talk to you,' he said. 'We'll go off and have–'

'Nonsense,' Archie interposed. He loathed having his plans changed. 'I made my arrangements, and I'm sticking to them. If Don wants to make his own plans, that's his affair. You can pay for your girl-friend's lunch yourself, Don,' he added unkindly, his son's smaller motives being as apparent to him as his deeper calculations. Ben's mouth twitched with amusement. He knew Don, too. 'I'm not footing the bill,' Archie went on. 'You two go off together and make your own lunch arrangements. Ben, you stay here and have Don's lunch. Come along now, we've been standing about long enough.' He rang for the lift, which had made several trips since he last summoned it, and shepherded them in. 'Be off with you,' he said to Don. 'You're nothing but a nuisance.' The lift doors shut on a view of an astonished Don and Nicola gazing blankly at them.

'Silly fellow,' Archie remarked. 'Thinks he can manipulate me. Forgets I'm his father, apparently. Come along now.' He herded them out of the lift and past the bar. 'Too late for sherry,' he announced firmly. 'Blame it on Don. Lunch at once, and hurry up about it. I wish you'd make it clear to Don, Jean,' he added disagreeably, 'that he's not to try and alter my arrangements like this. I won't have it. Sit down, sit down, don't stand about like a lot of ninnies. Only four of us, can't you sort yourselves out? Don't want me to tell you where to sit, do you?'

Jean sat down hastily, and pulled Hugh by the sleeve into the next chair. 'Oh dear,' she said. 'Darling, I am so *sorry*. That was very naughty of Don, and I'm extremely angry with him.' She looked at him with worried, puzzled eyes. She never quite knew how to deal with any of them.

Hugh looked back at the anxious, beseeching brown depths that he had known all his childhood, and suddenly found himself unable to present the cold unmoved front he had intended to display. This was dear old Aunt Jean being nice, and he could not fob her off with a pretence of non-caring, even if she was Don's mother. His own face came to sudden life, and he raised eyes to her that betrayed the hurt he had received, though he said only, 'They sprung it on me. I wasn't expecting it.'

'I am very angry with Don about this whole situation,' Jean said. 'It can't make for anyone's happiness.' This was not an aspect that had occurred to Hugh. 'I blame myself for starting it,' she went on. 'I encouraged him to drive her up that morning. But it never crossed my mind for an instant that he – oh, well, none of that helps now. Do you mind very much, Hugh?'

He swallowed, and stared at the table-cloth. What was he supposed to say to that? 'Not to worry, it's quite all right'? He looked up at her blunt features, screwed up with distress, and knew that he loved her and her homely ways. Throughout his childhood she had been an inadequate substitute for Annabel, and he had looked on her merely as that, a substitute, a stand-in. He had never been grateful to her for all she had done, but she had tried her best, just as she was trying now. It was others – Annabel, Don – who caused the trouble. Jean tried to comfort. He understood suddenly that she had become as irreplaceable as Annabel. So he told her the truth, without hedging. 'I did mind, yes. Very much, at first. It knocked me sideways.' He took a roll absentmindedly, tore it into half a dozen pieces, looked at them and pushed the plate away. 'Today,' he added, 'after I'd recovered from the shock of seeing them both, I – oh, I would have liked to have had a fight with Don, I suppose. About Nicola – what did I feel? I don't know, I simply don't know. It's a bit much of her, I think.'

'I think she wants a good smacking,' Jean said firmly.

Hugh smiled at her, a little ironically. Evidently, for Jean, despite her sympathy and her distress, this was all it amounted to – the children were upsetting each other, and one of them needed a good smacking. Jean's imagination had very definite limitations. Annabel, so much more selfish, would have understood more.

The soup plates were removed and replaced by plates of roast lamb. Roast potatoes and peas were served, red currant jelly passed round. The wine waiter poured burgundy.

'I ordered for all of you,' Archie explained. 'Can't waste time fiddling about. Don't usually drink at midday, thought we'd better have some wine, though. Strain. Cheer us up. Jean tense. Worried. Hugh too. No one worth it.' He brandished his knife and fork busily. 'Eat up,' he said.

Ben grinned. He always found Archie good value. He decided he had better play his part in improving the atmosphere. 'How's *Sea Goose?*' he enquired.

Archie was diverted at once, and looked up to hear Hugh's reply. He too had been worried about the outcome of Rodney's altruism.

'Bottom's foul,' Hugh said briefly, his mouth full.

'M-mm,' Archie agreed, also with a full mouth. He chewed and swallowed. 'So's *Moon Maid.* No good thinking you can get through the season, you can't. Morrow's having *Moon Maid* out this week. What are you doing about *Sea Goose*, then?'

'Well, I've been trying to scrape her myself, from the dinghy, but it's extraordinarily difficult to exert enough pressure. She really ought to come out.'

'Can't you do her against the old careening posts, between tides?' Ben asked. 'I'd come down and do her with you, if that would help. I could come down one night, and we could sleep on board. Shall I give you a ring, when I've worked out my days?'

'I'd be very grateful. I'm a bit dubious about managing by myself.'

'What you want to do,' Archie began, and gave them detailed instructions on the most effective method of scraping a ship's bottom between tides. He was as usual immensely efficient, and his advice was worth having. It lasted them through coffee, and on the last sentences he rose purposefully to his feet.

'Time to be off,' he said to Jean.

'We'll come down to the car with you,' Hugh said. They all descended again in the lift, and walked to the car parked round the corner. Archie paid no attention to the thanks he was receiving from Ben and Hugh for lunch, but ensconced himself comfortably in the driving seat and pulled on his gloves.

Jean as usual kissed Hugh maternally

167

before they parted. She was astonished to meet with a response from him. In the past he had always embraced her formally but coldly, his body like a stick in her arms. Today he laid his cheek against hers and gave her a warm hug. She felt quick tears start to her eyes, and said to Archie, as soon as they were away, 'We've got to do something about Hugh.'

'M'hm?'

'After all, he's just the same as if he were one of our own. I must say, at the moment I feel a great deal more fond of him than I do of Don.' She went off at a tangent. 'You remember,' she remarked, 'one of the things that wretched girl Nicola said when Don brought her for the week-end was how awful Hugh's room was. I think I'd better go down and see him.'

'Good idea,' Archie said imperturbably. 'You could go when I'm at the Edinburgh cardiology conference.'

This Jean did. She wrote to tell Hugh when she proposed to come, and asked him to book her a room. He did so, and decided her visit would be an excellent time to repay both the Warrs and the Calderwoods for some of their hospitality. He booked a table at the Rose and Crown for Saturday night and invited them all, and in addition persuaded the Warrs to come sailing on the Sunday. Jean was used to cooking on *Moon*

Maid, and he would lay in a great stock of food for her. All Jean's family took advantage of her in this way, without knowing that they were doing so, and she never thought of protesting.

Hugh began to look forward to her visit. It was nice of her to come down, he thought affectionately, and he greeted her sturdy figure with delight when her train came in. She was not, after all, staying at the Rose and Crown. The Calderwoods had vetoed it.

'But Hugh, of course she must come to us, I wouldn't dream of letting her stay in a hotel,' Margaret Calderwood had protested. 'It will be lovely to have her. We shall have so much to talk over – we trained together, you know.'

He had not known. Nor had Jock Calderwood, who said so when Hugh had gone. 'My dear, I didn't know you trained with Jean Ravelston, you've never said so.'

'Jean Buckley, she was. You must remember her.' Jock denied this. 'Such a nice creature,' Margaret went on. 'Though dreadfully ordinary, we all thought. We were flabbergasted when she simply picked up Archie Ravelston and walked off with him. Surely you remember that?'

'Sorry.'

'She was incredibly plain, of course, but I must say, she always looked so *good*. Not smug or anything, just gentle and kind and well-meaning. She had a sort of squashed face that was always very clean and school-girlish, and radiated amiability.'

'I expect Archie could read all that, and knew she'd make him a good wife, devoted and hard working. Trust a Ravelston.'

'I think you're very unfair always about the Ravelstons. I can't think why.'

'Can't you? I can. Envy.'

'But you've achieved exactly the life you want – haven't you?' She looked at him in alarm.

'I settled for what I could get, and be happy in, at an early age, and I've no regrets,' he said, smiling to reassure her. 'But Archie Ravelston was always able to leave me stand-ing. He was right out of my class. I don't exactly resent it, I don't want to be the sort of person Archie is. But one can't quite welcome being shown up as a second-rate brain, and I like to run the Ravelstons down when I have the opportunity. If you qualify at the Central, you become a little tired of hearing about the Ravelstons.'

She looked thoughtfully at him. 'So in a way, having a failed Ravelston on your staff was in the nature of a personal triumph?'

'I hope not,' Calderwood said, startled. 'You are a most uncomfortable person to have about, Margaret. You will take out my hidden feelings and brandish them at me.'

'Isn't that one of the things marriage is

for?' she asked bracingly, and he was reminded of the tough young physiotherapist he had married, thirty years earlier, who never shrank from telling her patients the unwelcome truth.

'It wasn't what I had in mind when I proposed to you,' he said gently.

'I daresay not. Nor in mine either. But we've tried to be honest with each other.'

'It's not being honest *with* each other I'm complaining about. It's being honest *for* each other. Sometimes I wonder what sort of person you see when you look at me – someone much nastier than anyone else imagines, I'm afraid.'

She smiled at him. 'I think you're very nice, darling,' she said comfortably. 'I just think it's a good plan not to let you settle down into a self-satisfied middle-age.'

'Have I shown any likelihood of doing that?' he asked, looking across at her from under his heavy brows.

'If it wasn't for me you would.'

'H'mph. I wonder what Archie's like in middle-age? It's years since I've talked to him. He used to specialise in being the only rude Ravelston. That was what he thought of as his distinction, do you remember?'

'Well, it is a distinction among the Ravelstons. I can quite understand how he felt about it.'

'Yes, but it's a very young attitude. I

171

wonder if it's survived into middle-age, or if he's mellowed?'

Margaret Calderwood, always forthright, asked Jean Ravelston. 'Is Archie still the only rude Ravelston, or has he mellowed?'

'Oh no,' Jean said. 'He's even ruder, I think. You see, they let him get away with it now. The students rather like it – he's a rude, outspoken professor, immersed in his research. They encourage him, you know.'

'Is he a strain to live with?'

'Archie?' Jean said in amazement. 'Oh no, Archie's the easiest person in the world to live with. It's the rest of the family I used to find such a strain.'

'Used to? Don't you any more?'

'Well, they aren't there any more. The old man frightened me, though I was quite fond of him in spite of that. Annabel I could never manage at all – she's Hugh's mother, you know. Completely charming, tremendously sophisticated, and utterly selfish. I could never cope with her. I tried not to be afraid of her, but I was always finding myself giving in to her when I hadn't meant to. I used to go away all churned up, not knowing what to do about it. She used to do the same thing to Hugh, of course, and it used to make me completely furious. He had no more idea of how to deal with her than I had. She was a bad mother,' Jean ended with hatred, baring her teeth at Annabel's memory.

'Good heavens, I've never seen you so ferocious,' Margaret said. 'You amaze me.'

'She was a wicked woman. She did her best to ruin Hugh.'

'You're rather melodramatic,' Margaret said doubtingly.

'You think I'm exaggerating. But it was heartrending to live through. She played havoc with that boy, and there was nothing I could do about it. And now she's cleared of to Switzerland, and she doesn't give a damn what happens to him.'

'You're very fond of Hugh, aren't you?'

'Well, he's like one of my own. After all, I had the upbringing of him from the time he was about ten, *that woman* couldn't be bothered with him – except when she suddenly decided to stir up trouble.'

'You know, I didn't realise he'd had any sort of a difficult childhood. Ben never mentioned it.'

'I don't suppose Hugh told even Ben about Annabel. He adored her, that was the trouble, you see. And then, I don't think he had the slightest conception of how exceptionally awful she was as a mother.'

'He never got on with old Sir Donald Ravelston, that I do remember Ben saying.'

'The old man was always unfair to Hugh. After Andrew died he was very much more difficult to deal with, you know. Andrew was like him, and they understood each other.

He was a clinician, too. The old man liked that. He never understood Archie going in for physiology, he didn't approve of it at all. He used to have frightful rows with him about it, and he used to attack me, too, saying I must stop him making a fool of himself and so on. Of course, Archie went his own way, he didn't care what his father or anyone else thought, he never has done. So I think the old man pinned his hopes on Andrew. Then he was drowned, and the old man got more and more embittered and withdrawn – especially after he retired – and he couldn't ever forgive Hugh for being Annabel's son, instead of a carbon copy of Andrew. It was a great pity, because they could have been such a comfort to one another. They were very much alike, only neither of them knew it.'

Margaret sighed. 'I'm afraid,' she pointed out, 'that it's too late for Hugh to have a career like Sir Donald's.'

Jean frowned. 'I know. Archie says he must stick to biochemistry now. He says he hasn't a hope in clinical medicine. And of course he can never get back to the Central, either. They don't forgive failure there. Aren't men awful?'

'Pig-headed and conventional, the lot of them. All afraid of stepping out of line.'

'It doesn't matter how good Hugh is, he's blotted his copybook. All the awful old men who count will make sure he never has a chance of a decent job.'

'When you think how short they are of good people, it's completely ridiculous. They wouldn't even let him back on the register, either, horrid old men. I had a fight with Jock about that. I said he ought to do something, you know, talk to some people and pull a few strings. He can, if he wants to. But he wouldn't. He said it was useless. Next year perhaps, but this year would be a waste of time. So I said to him, but it's a year of Hugh's *life*, and you won't even try. I think–'

'Archie was just the same. I had a go at him about it, and all he would do was mumble about biochemistry. At least Jock gave Hugh a job – Archie wouldn't.'

'Well, Jock didn't want to, you know. But he gave in, because Alec Ramsay began badgering him, as well as Ben.'

'I don't know, they call themselves doctors, but when it comes to dealing with each other, they seem to lack common humanity. I told Archie the least he could do was to take Hugh into his lab – I mean, they've got *acres* of benches, and hundreds of wretched chemists and physiologists and zoologists and mathematicians pottering about all day long, you'd think he could have found something for his own nephew. And it isn't as if Hugh hadn't a very good degree. If he had no medical qualifications, he'd still be better qualified than half these silly young men we have to invite to our revoltingly boring coffee parties.'

Margaret Calderwood couldn't help smiling to herself. She knew that neither Archie nor Jean had any small talk, and young science graduates were notoriously devoid of it, so the picture conjured up – especially to one who remembered Jean's coffee making – lacked attraction.

Jean was continuing. 'Archie said he couldn't because it would upset his father. As if he'd ever bothered before about upsetting the old man. Simply an excuse. He thought it would be a nuisance, and might be embarrassing. That was all. Except, of course, he was annoyed with Hugh.'

'Well,' Margaret said peaceably, 'it didn't matter, he–'

'It didn't matter because Jock found a job for him here. What if he hadn't?'

'Somebody would have done, in the end – especially if Alec Ramsay was ringing them all up. What a nice man he was. I was so sad to hear he'd died.'

'When Archie and I were first married, Ramsay was R.M.O. Now the old man's dead, and so is Alec Ramsay.'

'And Ben is R.M.O.,' Margaret said in tones of slight wonderment.

'We're all getting on,' Jean remarked.

'Ramsay will be missed at the Central. He was a humanising influence there – Jock agrees with me on that.'

'He was good to Hugh, when no one else was. He went out of his way to speak to him, too, at the memorial service. There aren't many in his position who would have taken the trouble. He was *kind.*'

'Hugh wasn't the easiest person to help, either,' Margaret remarked.

Jean's face fell. 'Has he been very tiresome?' she asked.

'I think Jock had quite a bit of difficulty with him. After all, it was only natural – you can't meet with a disaster like his and remain your best.'

'What *happened?*' Jean demanded anxiously.

'I don't know. Jock wouldn't discuss him. He said leave him alone, let him work it out for himself. But I kept on about him, because I knew Ben would want me to, and eventually Jock brought him out here one evening. And he was quite unapproachable, you know, very polite and all that, but hardly there at all.'

Jean sighed. 'That's how he always goes, when he's miserable. It does make things so *difficult.* Of course, that wretched girl Nicola was playing him up, I expect, as well.'

'Nicola?'

'Haven't you heard about her? Oh, my

dear, she's been such a nuisance all round. She's got her claws into my stupid Don, now.' Jean related the story, including the lunch after the memorial service.

'I see. Jock said the memorial service had upset Hugh. But I didn't know there was that complication. Actually – oh, I must have been wrong.'

'What?'

'I rather thought he was falling in love with Judith Warr.'

'Who's she?' Jean asked, sitting up alertly.

'Colin Warr's wife – you'll meet them tonight.'

'Oh,' Jean said in a dead voice. 'Oh dear, I can't bear it. He's not going to fall in love with a married woman now, and land himself up to the neck in new difficulties? Oh, how can he be such a *fool?*'

'It isn't quite like that,' Margaret said slowly. 'Anyway, I may be wrong about it. It was just an intuition I had. But – now, you're not to say a word, and don't, for heaven's sake, ever let on to Jock that you know, because he would be absolutely furious with me for telling you – but Colin Warr is very likely dying.'

'Oh. What of?'

'Hodgkin's Disease.'

'Oh. I see.'

'He's such a pet, I can't tell you how sad we all are. And Judith's devoted to him.

She's much younger than he is, it's his second marriage. But all the same ... in the long run, you know...' she couldn't bring herself to put what she was thinking into words, and simply added vaguely, 'I thought it might not be a bad thing at all.'

Jean sighed. 'I don't like it,' she said decidedly. 'Not after Nicola. I hope you're wrong. Simply another hopeless love.'

She watched Hugh surreptitiously throughout dinner that evening at the Rose and Crown, but reached no conclusion. Hugh was, after all, the host, besides being the youngest of them. He looked after them all, and seemed equally charming to Margaret Calderwood and Judith Warr. Jean decided Margaret's intuition was at fault – it often had been, in their student days, she remembered. She had a more practical worry to supersede her anxiety about Hugh's possible love affair. His lodgings. They were terrible. She did not mince her words to Margaret.

'How you can have thought it would do, Margaret, I simply can't imagine.'

'But Mrs Clifford's such a nice woman. I thought–'

'Have you ever been there?'

'Well, no, but I'm sure it's scrupulously clean, and Mrs Clifford is a most superior type of woman, you know–'

'If you haven't seen it you couldn't possibly understand. For one thing, it's in the most ghastly taste.'

Margaret thought the taste must be excruciating for Jean to notice it. In any case, she would hardly have thought that was vital. 'But after all,' she began.

'Oh, I know that's not important. But it was a shock to me, you see. It's incredibly garish, and there's–' she suddenly giggled '–there's plastic ivy all down one wall.'

'Plastic *ivy?*'

'Creeping all down one wall.'

'Good heavens, I would never have believed it of Mrs Clifford,' Margaret said, shaken.

'The wallpaper is imitation stone,' Jean giggled again. Then she pulled herself together. 'However, Hugh doesn't seem to mind at all, you're quite right there. He just thinks it's a good joke. And I agree the place is scrupulously clean. But the *noise.*'

'What noise?'

'Oh, everything. Never a moment's silence. It would drive me quite raving mad. There's traffic roaring past underneath the window, non-stop, people talking and arguing in the road and youths starting up their scooters, and hooligans shouting at girls, there's the television in the Cliffords' room underneath on at full blast, the child Sandra whining and crying and coughing – I know she can't help it, but she sounds quite disgusting in that tiny house – there's Mrs Clifford banging doors and shouting at them all and clattering about as if she was demented. And, my dear, every time anyone goes to the loo – it's next door to Hugh's room – the cistern simply drowns every other sound.'

'But–'

'I can't bear to think of Hugh going on living there, and what Annabel would say if she knew I can't imagine. I can't think what I'm going to do about it.'

'I'm sure we could quite easily find somewhere else for him,' Margaret said doubtfully, thinking how upset Mrs Clifford was going to be.

'That's just it. It's not the slightest use. He won't go.'

'If he's quite happy there, I don't see what you're fussing about,' Margaret said bluntly.

'My dear, he can't be happy there. It's simply this wretched child.'

'What, Sandra?' Margaret was surprised.

'Yes. He feels responsible for her, he says.'

'Responsible for her?'

'Oh, it's quite mad of him, and I told him so. Such an unattractive child, too. But I know exactly what's happened, it used to happen to me, too.' Before marriage, Jean and Margaret had been physiotherapists at the Central London Hospital. 'The more unattractive and hopeless they were, the more I used to feel it was up to me. It was always the hopeless misfits I got fond of,

181

didn't you?'

'There's something in what you say. It was usually old people with me.' And still is, she might have added. Margaret Calderwood gave her time liberally to the local old people's welfare committee, of which she was Secretary, and in addition gave a free service, through the committee, of home physiotherapy to old age pensioners in need of it. 'The more senile they were the more I wanted to help,' she now added. 'I remember being absolutely devoted to poor old dears who'd had strokes, mumbling and fumbling away. Well, I suppose I still am,' she admitted.

'With me it was always children,' Jean said. 'And it was always the pale little miseries I fell for. The ones who were never going to be any different – any more than this poor child Sandra is.'

'But what does Hugh think he's going to do about her?'

'He makes her do her exercises every morning, before he goes to the hospital.'

'Oh.'

'He's right, you see. It does make a difference to her. She *is* better because he forces her to drain her chest every morning, and gets her coughing over. She's getting more confidence in herself, he says. She's beginning to think she *can* manage her cough, and join in with other children. Oh, you

182

know how these children are. She can't be helped much, but if she can be encouraged to manage her own chest condition, her life is beginning to be tolerable. And Hugh thinks if he leaves there, she'll just slip back.'

'But surely Mrs Clifford–'

'She's too impatient. When she tries, it leads to tears – which is worse than not doing the exercises at all.'

'But she's such a sensible woman. I feel sure if it were explained to her – and she always *has* looked after Sandra herself. I mean, I'm sure it's very good of Hugh and rather surprising, I must say, I wouldn't have expected it of him–'

'He's always had a thing about small children.'

'I didn't know that. But in this case I can't help thinking that Mrs Clifford is perfectly competent.'

'Yes, well, I don't know,' Jean said with deliberate vagueness. Hugh had talked to her a good deal about Mrs Clifford. What he had said did not square at all with Margaret Calderwood's opinion of her daily woman. Hugh had warned Jean of this, and had added that he thought Margaret should be left in ignorance. 'It's natural Mrs Clifford should try to impress the Calderwoods, after all. And she can be very charming, when she wants to be. I find it quite hard, myself, to believe she's the same person I hear letting

183

rip downstairs, when I meet her putting on her charm. She seems so sincere. She is, I think. That's how she feels when there are people she wants to impress. Her relationship with the Calderwoods means a lot to her, you know. In a way, it's what makes up to her for her disappointment over Sandra.'

'But Hugh, that's terribly wrong. And very childish of her.'

'I just concentrate on Sandra, and leave Mrs C to look after herself – which she's entirely capable of doing.'

Jean had felt dissatisfied. She longed now to tell Margaret what a fool she was to be taken in by her daily woman to this extent. But decades of training by the Ravelstons were behind her. 'Leave well alone, my dear.' Often it was leave ill alone, she maintained. But they always came back to the same point. 'Don't stir up trouble.' She decided, reluctantly, that not only was there nothing she could do about Mrs Clifford, but nothing, either, about Hugh's lodging. He was determined to stay there.

In her preoccupation with the Cliffords, she forgot what Margaret had said about Judith Warr.

Here Margaret Calderwood was right. Hugh was in love with Judith. Unlike his other loves, this was an unwilling bondage. It had crept on him unnoticed, and he was still trying to escape it. But it held him securely.

However, he turned down Jean and Archie's invitation to spend Christmas with them at Cambridge. He knew Don would be there with Nicola – Jean had made a point of mentioning it – and he was by no means ready to face the two of them together. He might find that he no longer cared for Nicola, that there was nothing between them now. Or he might not. Either he would be battling with Don, to win her back from him, or she would mean little, and he would have to face the fact that he was bound to Judith Warr. He was not prepared for this.

He decided Christmas with Annabel would be less wearing. Annabel would have been furious if she had suspected that this was one of his motives for joining her.

VIII

Christmas in Switzerland made a complete break. Hugh flew out on Christmas Eve, exhausted by the pre-Christmas festivities in Brookhampton. There had been the nurses' dance, to which he had taken one of the technicians, then the lab party, at which he had carefully partnered a different technician, a party at the Calderwoods at which the entire lab staff were present, another dinner party there. This had been preceded by a party at the Cliffords, with cake and jelly and animal biscuits, so that even Hugh's usual vast appetite began to flag before the end of dinner. Then there had been a sherry party at the Warrs with half the grammar school present as well as the local doctors, and a carol concert in Brookhampton at which Judith had played Bach, and which he had attended with Colin. Before this he had given them both dinner at the Rose and Crown.

Annabel was delighted to see him. She had booked rooms for them all at a Mürren hotel. There was to be a big dance that night, Dominic and Sebastian were to stay up for it, and he himself must hurry and change. He joined them a little late in the bar, where Annabel and Simon were already in the middle of a large group. There were introductions, and more drinks all round, before they went in to dinner.

Dominic said nothing. He watched them all, and most particularly Hugh, through brown eyes like Annabel's. Sebastian was more lively, and, as far as Hugh was concerned, infinitely more tiresome. He never left Annabel alone. He interrupted her conversations with questions or assertions of his own, and whenever Hugh spoke he attempted a diversion. It was plain to everyone that he was determined at all costs to be the centre of attraction, and that he resented Hugh's arrival. He was nervy, infuriating, and often amazingly charming. In fact surprisingly like Annabel. Hugh found it impossible, in spite of his tiresome ways, to take him seriously.

Dominic was different. Dominic suffered. He was not seeking the centre of any stage. He simply loved Annabel. He was jealous of Hugh. He had reason to be, since Annabel gave him every cause. She had no time for either of her younger sons, now that Hugh had arrived – no time for Simon, either. Her eyes were on Hugh, and her talk was all of what she and Hugh might do together.

Simon was obviously inured to Annabel's behaviour, and he seemed to have no objection to her preoccupation with Hugh. Hugh thought he almost detected a certain amused relief in his attitude. But Dominic was hurt. He could not understand what had happened.

Dominic was now at a boarding school – some place Hugh had never heard of, in Switzerland, which Annabel asserted had done wonders for that poor boy of Pontevecchia's, who was such a problem at one time. He gathered that it was the type of school the Ravelstons would undoubtedly dub one of those crank places.

What had happened was obvious to him. He knew it all from his own childhood.

Dominic, returning home from school at the end of term, the new arrival into the family, had been made much of by Annabel, only to be dropped the instant Hugh, an even newer arrival, turned up. Dominic, of course, believed implicitly in Annabel's delight in his arrival, and he was unable to understand her withdrawal. He was trying to conceal this from himself, trying to work out some different answer.

All this went on in his hurt brown eyes as he constantly watched Annabel and Hugh together. Hugh wanted to beg him not to mind, to teach him how to take Annabel in his stride. But he had no opportunity. For Annabel too was jealous. Let Hugh's own eyes stray ever so slightly, let him be even momentarily engaged in talk of his own and fail to follow her lead, and she was up in arms. Amusingly up in arms, with a tinkling laugh, but clearly with the promise of trouble to come. Hugh was her darling boy, but only so long as he followed her path. No one would be more disappointed than Annabel if he failed to live up to her expectations.

He had not the heart to disappoint her. He was there for only ten days, he wanted at all costs to avoid a battle. He didn't, in any case, see what he could do about Dominic. He knew that if he himself had not been there Annabel would have found someone else in whom to be interested. This, of course, it came to him, was what Simon knew, and accounted for his air of relief.

This was Annabel. She required a constant supply of admirers. Dominic and Sebastian would have to adjust to the situation – it would be with them all their lives.

There was trouble, now, if Hugh went ski-ing. Annabel didn't ski. She preferred to sit in cafés drinking, first chocolate, then before-lunch aperitifs, then after-lunch coffee, then Russian tea, then before dinner aperitifs. That she remained so slim was astounding. The sole exercise she took was dancing after dinner, which she enjoyed until the early hours of the morning. She liked Hugh to escort her throughout her day. He liked to go ski-ing. There was no show-down, but he could see that there would have been if his stay had been longer. As it was he evaded the issue, by breakfasting before she appeared, going straight to the ski slopes, returning for lunch, and then spending the afternoon with her. She wasn't at all pleased by his absence during the morning, and made little semi-malicious jokes about it. He knew that to go ski-ing again in the afternoon would mean a rupture in their relationship. Even though this no longer brought the desolation it would have brought in childhood, he found it difficult to face. It was like this, he knew, for Dominic and Sebastian all the time. Hardly surprising that they were peaky, worried-looking children. His own childhood at Harbour Cottage, now that he could view it at second-hand, through the eyes of his two half-brothers, living their own version of it, no longer seemed an idyllic dream, a memory of golden days snatched away by fate – and Simon. It had been uncertain, full of the same doubts and stresses as Dominic and Sebastian's daily life. A difficult childhood, just as Annabel had been a difficult mother.

It had been, too, a life full of rows. This was what Annabel's family lived through now, and Hugh evaded them only by the skin of his teeth. If his stay had been a day longer, he suspected, he could not have kept the peace.

This was what only Annabel's family knew. Her friends thought her charming. She had hosts of them, everywhere, running in and out all day. She lived in the centre of a charmed circle. But in the smaller family circle she was a destroyer. She was, he suddenly saw, very like Irene Clifford, though they lived in different worlds. They were both tense energetic women, determined to shine, but unable to keep up the pose of charm and perfection inside the family. They were obstinately determined though, at all costs, to receive from inside the family the adulation that they could so easily win from outsiders.

For the first time it occurred to Hugh to wonder how his own father would have coped with Annabel. How had he managed her, during their brief married life? Had there been rows and reconciliations? They had both been young. Perhaps a stormy relationship had suited them then. What would it have become in the course of the years? From what he had heard about his father, Hugh could hardly imagine him settling down, as Simon had done, to play second fiddle to Annabel. Simon was apparently happy to do this. His only worries seemed to be concerned with Annabel's possible disappointments or frustrations. He had asked Hugh, for instance, if he need go ski-ing in the mornings. 'It upsets your mother,' he had pointed out. 'She has been looking forward so much to having you with her.'

'Good lord, she's got me in the afternoon and evening,' Hugh expostulated. 'And anyway she's never up before eleven at the earliest. I'm back at twelve. For heaven's sake, she can amuse herself for an hour, can't she?'

They both, of course, knew she could not. But all Simon said was, 'Well, it would please her so much if you were available in the morning too.'

'I'm sorry, she's out of luck,' Hugh said briefly. He was irritated by Simon. Bad enough to have Annabel on the verge of

191

sulks, without Simon appearing to share her belief that the world should revolve round her.

However, he did share her belief, and their marriage was a success, or generally accounted so. Annabel had found what she wanted in Simon. He not only gave her the cosmopolitan life she had yearned for, constantly brought interesting people home for her to entertain, but he never competed with her. He was happy for her to take him over, to rule their marriage. These were the only terms on which Annabel was able to love. Her world had to be peopled by charming puppets, of whom she pulled the strings.

As a child, Hugh had rebelled against this take-over bid. He had loved her deeply, but he had refused to be her creature. He had, for instance, gone sailing, despite her obvious displeasure. He began to understand that his rebellion had brought unavoidable consequences. Annabel had never succeeded in dominating him more than intermittently. So she had dropped him. At last he saw the mechanism, saw that it had been inevitable – and his salvation.

No wonder, though, that he still carried the conflict in him between Ravelston and Annabel. No wonder, too, that Annabel had detested the Ravelston in him. It all seemed so obvious now, and with the understanding came a lightening of his spirits. Knowledge grew, and he felt free for the first time in his life. Free to be himself, no longer what others wanted. Knowledge grew, like the tide spreading up the estuary, flooding through the creeks and inlets, outlining clearly the shape of the land, where before had been mud and marsh. It grew as inexorably and yet as gently as the flood tide, so that now he could hardly imagine that he had not known it at all, seen it all, for years past.

But look where Annabel had led him, he thought sadly. All those parties and the Alfa-Romeo, that had been Annabel in him. That had been Don's rotten little show-off. It was the Ravelston in him that had made him combine this superficiality with medicine and hard work and the realities of the wards and the clinics. These two lives in collision had brought about the final failure. Now it was his failure, that he, nearly all Ravelston, had to live with. Somehow he had to remake his life, and he had to remake it against the reasonable doubt of those who knew him well. What sort of faith would he have in Dominic or Sebastian in similar circumstances? It was all clear to him now. What remained hidden was the future. Had he to find a new road of his own? Were all doors in medicine closed? Was it futile to try to continue? He could not tell.

He could even begin to be fair to Annabel, now. Something came to him from her that was valuable. Part of what she constantly asserted about the Ravelstons was true. They were cold, calculating, ironic. He had something in him from Annabel that was warm and responsive. This, presumably, was why his heart was in the wards, and not in the laboratories.

However, it was the laboratory at Brookhampton to which he had to return in the New Year. Despite the imperfection of the holiday with Annabel, it was hard to return to the bleak wet days of a cold dull January in Brookhampton and the daily drudgery of repetitive tests. Hard, too, to tolerate the noise of the Cliffords' tiny house in the dark evenings.

Slowly the days drew out, the daffodils came, the Cliffords' lilac budded again and flowered beneath his window. Sandra Clifford had weathered this winter better than usual, had missed school less frequently, had acquired some interests of her own. Maxwell Okiya's chief had suggested he write her case up. He had pointed out to Okiya that such a paper would be a help to him in his career, and Hugh knew this to be true. He helped him with the account, with the biochemical details and explanations. They wrote it in the evenings, in the Dog and Duck, in Hugh's noisy room at the Cliffords, and, as spring crept unwillingly towards summer, on board *Sea Goose*. When it was ready for publication Okiya announced that he expected Hugh's name on the paper as co-author. Hugh promptly refused. Okiya was adamant. He threatened not to send it off at all unless Hugh agreed. They tussled for a week, by which time it had dawned on Hugh that Okiya was in earnest. He gave in, and the paper went to the editor of *Acta Paediatrica – An Unusual Case of Cystic Fibrosis of the Pancreas, by Maxwell Okiya, M.B., B.Ch., D.C.H. and H.D. Ravelston.* Hugh refused to have his M.A. added to his name. 'All or nothing,' he said, 'and it certainly can't be all, so it had better be nothing.' The paper was to cause a small stir at the Central, where they began discussing Hugh Ravelston's future again.

Hugh himself was fully occupied with Warr's work on the metabolic aspects of hypertension. He put in extra time on this in the evening, when he wanted to complete a series of tests, or to finish some calculations in the peace and quiet of the laboratory when the staff had departed. Then there was varnishing and painting to be done on *Sea Goose,* checking the rigging, tinkering with the engine.

At Easter, he was invited by Annabel to Switzerland and by Jean to Cambridge. However, he accepted neither invitation, but instead went sailing with Ben. As they had feared, the week-end was cold, wet and miserable, and they spent it muffled to the eyebrows in all their sweaters, thick socks, trousers over jeans, oilskins over the lot, towels round their necks, gloves on their freezing hands. The wind blew, the sea was grey and uninviting. Getting the mainsail up was hell, and getting it down again worse hell.

They made Yarmouth in the Isle of Wight before the wind reached gale force, had an enormous meal in the Bugle and a great deal to drink, rowed back to *Sea Goose* and climbed into their sleeping-bags, where they lay listening to the wind howling and twanging through the rigging.

The next day the gale force wind still blew, and they decided to stay where they were. By Sunday, it had blown itself out, and they sailed down to Poole through a choppy sea, and anchored just before dark. They cooked themselves a large and splendid meal from the stores they had laid in at Yarmouth – pork chops, bacon, sausages, tomatoes, chips, apple sauce out of a tin, and a bottle of wine from the Bugle. Then they went to bed, and were up at four in freezing moonlight to catch the first of the flood for the return to Brookhampton.

The weather, to everyone's irritation – all the talk was of waterlogged holidays in caravans, tents, or seaside hotels full still of affronted winter residents – turned perfect for the next week. However, this gave Hugh a chance to dry out the sails and the gear, and restow. He often, now, had company while he worked on *Sea Goose*. Sometimes Okiya, who said sailing was too cold a pastime for Northern latitudes, but who enjoyed pottering about on board for an hour or two as an antidote to the residents' mess, provided he was given a mug of hot coffee. Or there were the girl technicians, only too eager to be asked aboard, and most of them pleasant and companionable. He found none of them exciting, but he liked to have a girl about to hold things, brew up, and generally boost his morale by being at his beck and call. He was cautious, though, these days, and had what amounted to a strict rota for his invitations. None of them could have said that she was sought after by Hugh Ravelston more often than any of the others, and he treated them all impartially, with a sort of affectionate reserve that fascinated them.

It was not Nicola whom he was trying to forget, or put out of his mind, though. It was Judith Warr.

Here he knew he had no hope. Judith appeared fond of him. She was used to having him around with Colin, she enjoyed sailing with him, she had been quite happy to let him escort her to concerts when Colin had appointments he could not cut. They had fun together, enjoyed one another's company, they were the same age. But Judith, Hugh was convinced, thought of him as being ten years younger than herself. He was Colin's young research assistant, a nice enough boy, and useful.

So there it was. There was nothing for him to hope for, even had he been able to wish for any future with Judith that excluded Colin. He knew it was only too likely that in a few years' time Colin would have died, but he could only dread this outcome. If – or when – it came, he hoped that he would be able to be of some help to Judith. She knew very little about medicine – about as much as Colin knew about music – and Colin would not allow her to be told of the danger he was in.

'I won't have it hanging over her head,' he had said on numerous occasions. So Judith was content in their marriage, and saw no small cloud on the horizon, not even the size of a man's hand.

All Hugh had to do, as he frequently told himself, was to get over his feelings for her. He had recovered from his love for Nicola, which had been genuine enough at the time. Now it seemed pale and thin compared with the desire and pain that swept him when Judith made one of her lovely movements. She had a trick of gesturing wildly with her supple long-fingered hands, in emphasis as she talked, and again and again he had to fight down an impulse to catch these hands as they flew out, to hold them tightly while he forced her to pay attention to him. His bones longed to dissolve into hers. The turn of her head fascinated him, and he wanted to handle her heavy tawny hair, to touch the soft skin of her cheek and feel the bone beneath, or simply to draw her to him in what he found it hard to believe would not be an inevitable coming together.

But there was nothing inevitable about it. Even if she had had any wish to respond to him, there was nothing they could have done.

For the first time in his life, Hugh was, though driven by desire and longing, willing to let matters stand as they were. He hoped that when one day the hard truth was brought home to her that Colin was dying, he would have an accepted place in her life. More than this he did not expect, and he saw with bleak clarity that friendship at such a time was unlikely to lead to love.

This time was nearer than they knew. Colin had become steadily more short of breath. For weeks Hugh had watched him panting as he reached the laboratory, after a slow climb up the stone stairs that Hugh himself took at a run. He had lost a stone and a half in weight since Hugh first met him. He was a great hulk of a man, now, tired and breathless, only the unquenchable vitality shining out of his pale eyes to remind them that the same Colin Warr they had all known was still with them, though his body was breaking up round him.

These days, he would scratch insatiably. Hugh watched him, as he slumped on a stool in the laboratory, and began totting up the months. For it was likely, now, to be months, no longer years. Jock Calderwood had forced him to see Taylor – or rather, to be accurate, had brought Taylor to see him, cross and grumpy in outpatients at the end of his clinic. Taylor had examined him, and new X-rays were taken.

The results were as bad as they had feared. His lungs were involved. Much against his will he was admitted for a second course of deep X-ray treatment, lasting for six weeks. During this time he was morose and bad-tempered. He felt ill, he was deeply depressed, and he was worried about Judith's future. Here he was in conflict. He wanted to think of her – still in her middle twenties – as happy and satisfied in a future that he could not share. This meant remarriage and a new life. He tried to face this, but, sick and sad himself, he wanted all her devotion, all her tenderness, all her care. He wanted her to cherish him and him only. He watched her and Hugh together and fought a battle with himself, alternately swept by jealousy and praying that they would care for one another, that Hugh would take over, that there would be no desolate break in her life.

They both found him extraordinarily difficult to deal with, at one moment packing them off to the cinema together, at the next making it impossible for them to leave.

He threw himself, too, into his research project, and demanded superhuman efforts from Hugh. He appeared to expect results in half the time, sitting propped up in bed with foolscap sheets all over the place, complaining bitterly and demanding his secretary.

The summer days slid by half-noticed. Hugh had little time now for *Sea Goose*, though he continued to sleep on board when he had the opportunity, just to keep in some sort of touch with another world. But he was in the laboratory early and late working, and Colin was always urging him to take Judith out. There was nothing he liked better, except that he was so short of time. But Colin was worried about Judith's state of mind, and did not like her to be alone too much. Here he, oddly, forgot that not having been given his diagnosis, her state of mind was one out of touch with reality. She missed Colin, and she had worried of course, at the news that he needed another course of deep X-rays. To her this form of treatment meant cancer, and she had asked him outright if he had a growth.

'If you knew more about medicine, darling,' he had said easily, 'you would know that this treatment is given for any number of conditions besides cancer. Skin diseases, for one thing,' he suggested happily, knowing that one ray was the same to her as another. X-ray, ultra-violet, infra-red – Judith was scientifically idiotic, and to her they all came out of machines and were something to do with electricity. If he had told her the electric fire gave off X-rays when it was unplugged, she would have accepted it.

But she was not as easily reassured as he assumed, and asked Hugh if Colin had lung cancer. 'He says not, but if he has, I want to know,' she said fiercely, her eyes, frowning, on the road ahead. She was driving him in Colin's car to a concert.

'Lung cancer?' Hugh queried, to gain time. 'What makes you think that?'

'His breathing has gone to pot, he's lost all that weight, and he's having X-ray treatment. That's what they give cancer patients, isn't it? Of course, he says it's used for other things, too. But I want to *know*. Has he got lung cancer? You've got to tell me, Hugh.'

'He has not got lung cancer,' Hugh said, relieved that he could tell the truth, yet knowing that basically he was deceiving her.

'Swear.'

'Colin has not got lung cancer, and that's the truth,' Hugh said. 'You'll have him home in a week or two,' he added. 'Large as life and full of beans.'

'Do you think so? He isn't going to die, all alone in that beastly little room?'

'You'll have him home in a week or two. He'll begin putting on weight again, and in a month from now he'll be driving this car himself.'

'You've lifted a load off my soul,' she said simply, and dropped one hand from the wheel to clasp his. 'Thank you, Hugh darling. I believe you, and I can't tell you how much better I feel.'

He felt as if he had betrayed her irretrievably. He turned his head away, unseeing. But what else could he have done? This was Colin's decision, and Colin's choice.

What he had said was, of course, factually correct. Colin was home in a fortnight, he did begin to put on weight, and he took up the threads of his practice again. His first action was to order Hugh off on a fortnight's holiday.

'You're exhausted,' he announced, lying in a deck chair in the cottage garden. 'Thin as a rake, great hollows under your eyes, air of nervous tension. Get on board *Sea Goose* and disappear for a couple of weeks.'

Hugh muttered vaguely. He was tired, of course, but he wasn't sure that he wanted to go off at a moment's notice.

'Pull out while the going's good,' Colin advised. 'I may not be so keen to let you go in a week or two. At present I'm feeling guilty. I know you've been doing two men's work for the last three months. But the crisis is over – I admit I thought I'd had my chips, and I didn't give a damn if you worked yourself to a standstill as long as the project moved and I could get some idea of how it was going to pan out.'

'Col–' Hugh began, and stopped.

'Well?'

'Are you – don't you think – when are you going to tell Judith?'

'Mind your own bloody business.' Warr's face darkened and grew heavy.

'She's asked me, you know.'

'Asked you what?'

'If you had lung cancer.'

'H'mh. Girl's not a bad diagnostician, for a pianist, is she? What did you say?'

'That you hadn't.'

'What else?'

'Said you'd be home and putting on weight and running your practice in September.'

'Accurate fellow, aren't you?'

'Said to be a Ravelston characteristic,' Hugh said glumly, pulling up handfuls of grass as he lay sprawled on the lawn.

'Stop destroying my lawn, and leave me to manage my own wife.'

This hurt, and Hugh flushed.

'Oh, I'm sorry,' Warr said at once. 'But let's leave the girl in peace, shall we, while we can? She'll know soon enough. Just go on lying, if you have to, there's a good chap.'

There was nothing more Hugh could do about it.

'Anyway,' Warr added, 'it's time you got shot of my worries. Lose yourself for a fortnight, and get a different outlook on life.'

Hugh did just that. He didn't even wait to telephone Ben, he simply went aboard *Sea Goose* with a few stores, cast off, and sailed, as they had done at Easter, for Yarmouth. Arrived there, he put out mooring lines, and then cooked himself a huge meal of bacon, tinned sausages, baked beans, fried bread, and about a quart of coffee. He had intended to go ashore afterwards to the shops, but instead went to sleep. He woke after dark, feeling hungry again. So he had bread and cheese and beer, sitting in the cockpit in his thick sweater, watching the harbour at night, the ships going by in the Solent, and the lights on the water.

In the morning he cooked more beans and bacon – there was little else left on board to eat – washed up everything from the night before, put his sleeping-bag in the sun on deck to air, washed and shaved. Then he tidied ship and went ashore to telephone Ben, who he knew was due for leave, and who promised to join him in two days' time. Meanwhile he stocked up with food and drink, and his respect for Jean, who saw to all this on *Moon Maid* without batting an eyelid, rose considerably.

When Ben arrived, they sailed out through the Needles, and had an exhilarating cruise down to St Peter Port and back, just making Brookhampton for Ben to catch the first Waterloo train, which would get him to the Central for the day's work. Ben was now Resident Medical Officer, and had a great deal of detail on his plate, about which he seemed quite undisturbed. Hugh himself cleared up on board, and went back to the Cliffords for a bath and breakfast, before going along to the laboratory at nine. He was completely refreshed and ready for anything.

Warr's project now began to move at a tremendous pace, with two of them on it again, and both of them determined to achieve results.

Okiya's paper came out, and even this gave Hugh some pleasure. The following day Ben rang him. 'You've caused quite a stir with your nice little paper, suddenly appearing out of the blue,' he said. 'You might have told me, I must say. People keep coming up and asking me about it.'

'It's not my paper, it's Okiya's.'

'That's not what they think here.'

'Well, it is. It's meant to help Max's career. All I did was a bit of chemistry on the side.'

'You can tell that to the marines. Good God, d'you think I can't recognise your impeccable literary style by now? And so can everyone else.'

'OK, so I tidied up old Max's English here and there – it's apt to be a little Victorian, if he's left to himself. That's how they taught him to express himself when writing essays, apparently. But it's his ruddy paper. The child's his patient.'

'His ruddy landlady, too, I suppose?' Ben asked sarcastically.

'What?'

'Have you forgotten telling me all about the Clifford child? Come off it, Hugh. Anyway, let me tell you this. I don't give a damn about Okiya's career. But if it's so effortless, and all you did was a bit of chemistry on the side, you'd better go round the Brookhampton General doing a few more bits of chemistry for all the clinicians you can lay hands on. Because this paper's done you a lot of good.'

'Ridiculous. However, I can do with it, even if unearned.'

'You'd better come and show yourself, looking clean and tidy and well-scrubbed, and start collecting some nice testimonials from all quarters.'

'Raspberries, more likely.'

'No, I'm perfectly serious. They're beginning to feel ashamed of themselves. They realise you copped a packet, and it's at last dawned on them that they ought to have been there behind you fighting, not trampling on you.'

'I don't feel trampled on,' Hugh said curtly.

Ben laughed. 'No Ravelston ever does. But you'll admit that you were showing slight signs of wear at one stage.'

'I admit it. In fact, on second thoughts I admit I was trampled on, and had to be picked up and dusted down by B.G. Calderwood, without whom I should never have reached the giddy heights to which I have now attained.'

'Put on your nice black suit and your – um–' he paused in time to bite back the words 'your Central tie.' That wouldn't do at all. He went on with hardly a pause (only Hugh would have noticed it, but he knew what the unuttered words had been) '–your Garside tie, and show yourself among the seats of the mighty. Then you ask them to sign on the dotted line.'

'I don't think I can.'

'You've got to.'

It went against the grain. In the end he funked it, and wrote a few polite notes. Others were working for him, though. Jock Calderwood went up to London and made the rounds. Even Archie, up for a meeting of the Royal Society, decided to make a few calls on Hugh's behalf. Rodney too was doing the rounds. He had returned from the Antarctic, and paid his first visit to Brookhampton, where he met Hugh in the Dog and Duck.

They hit one another on the shoulders – the Ravelstons' notion of extreme affection – and laughed for no reason.

'If you had only rung to say you were coming, I would have met you, and we could have had what passes here for a smashing meal at the Rose and Crown. Can you stay overnight?'

'Sorry, nothing doing. An appointment tomorrow morning.'

'How about having a snack here, then? I always do.' He went off to order this, while Rodney stretched his own legs to the blaze, and relaxed.

Hugh came back with French bread, cheese, celery, and beer, set everything down neatly on the table. He had always been extraordinarily deft with his fingers, curiously soft and gentle with everything he touched, whether a patient, a girl or a glass of beer – or, Rodney would have said at one time, the wheel of a car. Distress swept over him. Hugh's gentle touch was unlikely to be used ever again on a patient. The waste of it all. Then he pulled himself together. This was sheer sentimentality. He could take his deftness of touch into the laboratories, and make good use of it. There would be no waste then. Hugh had a good brain, possibly even an original one.

Hugh's mind at this moment was far away from his own troubles. 'You'll want to look over *Sea Goose*,' he announced, sitting down. He watched Rodney's eyes light up, and smiled. 'Not to worry,' he said, reading the anxiety there as well as the excitement, and patting him kindly, avuncularly. 'She's in good shape. I haven't smashed her up for you.'

He watched the relief flood Rodney's give-away countenance, and grinned. 'Pity you can't stay till tomorrow,' he remarked. 'We could have gone for a sail – I'd have taken a few hours off.' He considered. 'What about the week-end? Could you come down, and then we could sail her round to East Callant?'

'Can't manage the week-end either,' Rodney said regretfully. 'I haven't properly seen the family yet, and I promised Emma nothing should interfere with our week-end. No appointments, no visitors. You can have *Sea Goose* for a bit longer, Hugh.' He smiled. 'I've no time to sail her myself just now.'

'I could sail her round to East Callant for you,' Hugh offered.

'What for? For Morrow to lay her up? Much good that would do either of us. Keep her here, until I sort myself out. Then we'll see. I can probably pop down for a sail in a week or two, anyway.'

Hugh glanced at his watch, and then at Rodney's beer. 'Drink up,' he urged. 'We can go aboard now. There's time to put in a couple of hours before the nine-thirty. We'll have coffee on board.' He began returning their assortment of plates and glasses to the bar, and then they set off, like a couple of schoolboys.

'Takes twenty minutes flat,' Hugh stated as they pounded the pavements. 'I know to the minute. That at least is one advantage you have at the Brookhampton General that you don't get at the Central. Twenty minutes walk and you're on board. Jam on it, really.'

They came to a wide old-fashioned street, tiny houses set back in Victorian terraces, the whole dilapidated and slum-like in the lamplight.

'Nearly there,' Hugh announced. They turned a couple of corners, and there was the river, placid in the light from the lamps along the narrow embankment. They went through an iron gate to a small jetty, where the water slapped against stone, and climbed down a ladder to the dinghy. Hugh cast off, and slipped the oars into the rowlocks. There was hardly any wind, just a breeze to ruffle the surface of the water. Hugh rowed steadily, round a bend in the river, glancing over his shoulder from time to time, and then, with absolute precision, standing on his oars at the moment she came into Rodney's view. *Sea Goose*, lying on her mooring, mast high in the night sky. The most beautiful creature in Rodney's life, his great love.

Rodney stared, and then gave a deep sigh of content. Hugh began to row again, and they came alongside. Hugh clambered aboard, made the dinghy fast. Rodney followed him, stood looking about, ahead to the bows, astern, where the mooring line at this state of the tide, was taut. Hugh was occupied in removing the cockpit cover, but Rodney, standing in a daze by the mast, never noticed and made no attempt to help him. He failed to spot the expression of gentle amusement on his cousin's face, and would have been considerably shaken if he had seen it – Hugh had never looked at him like that in his life before. But this was unknown to both of them.

Hugh busied himself in the cabin, and when Rodney at last came out of his trance, and joined him there, he found the lamp alight and the kettle singing. Hugh looked up, as Rodney swung himself down. The light from the oil lamp deepened his eye sockets and hollowed his cheeks, pared away all but the essential structure. It was a man's face that Rodney saw, no longer a boy's, and the eyes regarded him with an unfathomable expression which startled him. It was as though Hugh were looking at him with some tolerance, as if he were half-amused and half-touched by Rodney's reactions. 'Go ahead and stroke her,' he remarked with a grin. 'I shan't jeer.'

Rodney smiled a little apologetically, but moved briskly round the cabin, opening lockers, fingering their contents, sniffing the air with mingled suspicion and content. Hugh was occupied in pouring water on to Nescafe, and adding Marvel. He handed Rodney a mug, saying, 'All out of a tin, but you must be used to that by now.'

'M-m, thanks,' Rodney assented vaguely, and went out to the cockpit with his steaming mug. The wind played over the water, the ripples flashed and dipped in the moonlight, all the infinitesimal sounds of *Sea Goose* on her mooring was music in his soul. Below, in the lighted cabin, he could see Hugh in profile as he leant back on the bunk, head tilted to stare upwards through the hatch towards the night sky. Now he looked relaxed and at peace, and Rodney guessed at once that to be afloat brought him tranquillity. So it had always been for Rodney himself, but until now, although they shared the struggle and exhilaration of sailing, they had never shared its peace. Hugh had been too young. He had felt no need for tranquillity. Striving, effort, achievement – these had been his life.

Thank God, Rodney thought, that he had

followed his instinct and trusted *Sea Goose* to Hugh during those difficult years. He had looked after her as obsessionally as Rodney would have done himself. There had been no need to worry.

'You've looked after her well,' he remarked.

'Oh lord, yes. I've fussed over her like an old hen. I was staggered you trusted me with her.'

'I was a bit staggered myself. But it was all I could think of to do. Not much, but something, I hoped.'

'A hell of a lot. *Sea Goose* kept me going. Not only that, but–' he hesitated, tipped the coffee about in his mug.

'But what?'

'Well – it came at a critical moment, your letter about *Sea Goose*. I'd just about had enough, you know. I must have been in a sort of trough of futility. I suppose I was suffering from reaction, after all the uproar. Mainly, I think, I was tired, and – well, extremely despondent, to put it mildly. But I hadn't any initiative to start anything, I was drifting along miserably feeling sorry for myself. Then your letter came, and I was at once plunged into activity. No more time for depression.' He stood up, and his head came through the hatch. He rested his elbow on the coaming, and leant his forehead on his hand. Rodney studied him with surprise. He had always, of course, been good looking, but now he had acquired a distinction he had lacked previously. He had an unmistakable look of their grandfather.

'It was the beginning of real life again,' he was saying, looking out across the river. 'The beginning of understanding that life went on. So you see, I'm grateful not only for the boat, but also for – for getting me cracking again.'

They were both embarrassed at this.

'I wish I'd been able to do more,' Rodney said briefly.

'So do I,' Hugh agreed, with a sudden smile. 'But it was a good thing you weren't, you know. Time I learnt to stand on my own two feet.'

'Perhaps. Still, I would have liked to have been able to help.'

'I've just told you how much you did.'

'Was it – did you – did you mind – did you have a very bad time, Hugh?'

'Lonely, mainly. And of course I was furious with myself. Everyone else, too.'

'And now?'

'Now? Oh, I don't know. I've adapted. I think so. After all, it's not a bad life, here. As long as I don't try to put the clock back. Occasionally, of course, I long to be back in the old days, back in my–' he suddenly snorted, threw his head back, and laughed with genuine amusement '–my undoubtedly gilded youth. *You* know. Mind you, I've changed a good deal, I wouldn't be the same person if I was suddenly translated back into it. And just as well, I should say. But of course I can't help longing for the old opportunities to return.'

They won't, Rodney thought, his heart sinking. Not ever. Don't let's kid ourselves about that.

'They won't,' Hugh stated flatly. 'No one knows that better than I do. But you see, I still hanker, from time to time. After Ben's been down, I start again. I'm delighted to see the old boy, and God knows what I would have done without him, but I'm all churned up after he's gone. He's R.M.O., now, you know. That's a job I might have had.'

'You still wish you were back at the Central, then?'

Hugh shrugged. 'No good wishing. I never shall be. But it's true, I can't quite leave the idea alone.'

Rodney was torn by pity and his own helplessness. Because Hugh was right. Whatever happened to him in the future, however well he succeeded in mending his broken career – and now Rodney knew that, contrary to what their grandfather had believed, Hugh had the capacity and the endurance, the toughness, in fact, to rebuild his life – he would never get back to the Central.

'It's a silly wish, anyway,' Hugh said

lightly, almost as though he knew how much Rodney was distressing himself. 'Time I grew out of it. It's a delayed adolescence, that's all. And there are compensations – as you can see for yourself, this minute – in being down here, as Calderwood has always pointed out. After all, he chose to come here – they would have kept him if they could. But he says he's never regretted his choice. Still, there's a slight difference between being chucked out and going in search of new values.'

'Has he found them?'

'I think he always had a saner view of life than most of us. Achievement doesn't matter to him. All he wants is to live his life in the way he wants. It's a very adult viewpoint. Work and play for their own sake, not for the status the world gives you, the rewards that may come your way. Just a good day's work, which he enjoys as much as a hobby, and for the rest of the time the open air, the sea, his boat, his family, friendships, books. There's no competitiveness in him.'

'That's the state to attain, if you can,' Rodney agreed.

'It's an excellent ambition, in fact, to strive to be without ambition,' Hugh suggested. 'The trouble with me is that I'm far from that happy state. I used to be the prize-winner, the one who was admired. I used to belong to a little tiny world where everyone knew about my achievements. I haven't learned how to be a nonentity and be happy. I need to learn to do the job for its own sake, not for the applause. But I'm eaten up with competitiveness still. Oh well – we'd better go ashore if we're going to catch your train.'

As they walked to the station, Rodney suggested that Hugh should come up to London for the week-end. 'Because I can't possibly get down here for at least the next two week-ends,' he said, 'and we've hardly begun to talk. Can you spare a week-end away from *Sea Goose?*' He smiled. 'I don't suppose I would, in your shoes.'

'I thought Emma said no visitors?' Hugh pointed out with a grin.

'Good lord, she doesn't count you.'

'Don't be so sure. Anyway, she won't have to. I simply haven't the time to spare just now. We're a bit pushed at the moment, you see.'

There was no opportunity to explain more about Warr's illness and his research project, as they reached the station, and the train was signalled. Hugh saw Rodney to his carriage, shut the door on him, and almost immediately the train left. Hugh raised a hand in salute, and turned back to the barrier.

Rodney watched him go, as the train slipped along the platform. Something had to be done about Hugh's future. He must talk to people. He couldn't be allowed to spend the years mouldering in Brookhampton. He began to wonder if the Central was irrevocably closed to him. As a clinician, yes. But a research post, in the laboratories? That might be a possibility. He must take soundings.

IX

Hugh was making the now familiar journey from Waterloo to Brookhampton. He had never made it in such tearing spirits. He could hardly contain himself, and continually found his gaze had left the *Lancet* open on his knee and was blindly on the suburbs flashing past the window, an idiotic grin on his face.

His name was to be restored to the register. He would never know whether this was the result of the testimonials he had dutifully submitted, saying, presumably, that he was careful, sober and industrious, whether it was the effect of the lobbying of Jock Calderwood, Archie Ravelston and latterly Rodney. He hardly cared. The result was what mattered. Whether the decision had much to do with his work in Brookhampton, or whether it was taken because of a single piece of

information unearthed by Ben – information, which, if it had been available two
years earlier, would certainly have altered the
course of events – he could not tell.

Ben had met Brian Thompson, a former
registrar at the Central who had recently
returned from a fellowship in the States.
They had begun to talk about Hugh, and
Brian had at once said that he had been
responsible for referring Angela Carlton to
Vanstone's clinic, and that he knew for a
certainty that Hugh had neither seen her
nor known that she had attended. Brian
himself had taken her straight in to Vanstone, and he was surprised to learn that
there was any record of her attendance, as
he had been under the impression that
Vanstone was seeing her privately. Exactly
like Vanstone, though, they both agreed, to
fill in all the forms meticulously.

Angela had at that time been a girl-friend
of Brian's. She had been complaining about
headaches, sleeplessness, loss of weight, and
so on. Their affair was at that time breaking
up – as all Angela's affairs did – and Brian
thought these complaints were more a
means of putting pressure on him than a
sign of genuine ill-health. Angela wanted to
travel to New York with him as his wife.

Brian had seen Vanstone, whose registrar
he had been a year earlier, and had asked
him if he would see Angela. Vanstone had

told him to bring her along to the clinic one Thursday afternoon. This he had done. Vanstone had seen the girl, had been of the opinion that there was nothing in her symptoms, had referred her to her own general practitioner, and had washed his hands of the matter. She was neurotic and attention-seeking, he had told Brian Thompson, who had then cleared off to the U.S.A, his mind full of his fellowship. Neither of them had thought further about Angela Carlton.

Challenged, Vanstone asserted, as he had stated previously when the question had first been raised, that he had no recollection of the occasion or the patient. This seemed likely. He saw at least fifty patients a week at the Central alone.

Only Angela remembered, and had made use of the visit to discredit Hugh when the opportunity occurred – though quite possibly, Ben considered, even she had intended only to give Hugh a bad name among his seniors, rather than to break his career.

Hugh shrugged. This was all in the past. All that mattered now was that he was back on the register, he could practise again. A load had been lifted.

If his grandfather had been alive, he would have known that this was not all that mattered. With his fanaticism about the Ravelston name, he would have insisted on clearing it publicly – as publicly as it had been discredited. He would have put Blennerhasset on to the case again, with an action for damages, perhaps.

But Sir Donald Ravelston, with his worldly knowledge and his pig-headed stubbornness about the Ravelstons, was dead. Neither Hugh himself, nor Archie, nor Rodney, thought of any action of this sort. They were all relieved that matters had turned out to be not so bad after all. The last thing they thought of doing was stirring up a lot of mud.

As soon as he knew the result, Hugh telephoned Ben to pass on the news. Then he caught the next train back to Brookhampton. Ben had tried to persuade him to stay in London for a celebration dinner, but Hugh had refused. Ben, who was in the middle of a clinic, had been unable to argue the point.

At Brookhampton, Hugh grabbed the station taxi. While they were still in the centre of the town he stopped the driver while he dived into a wine merchant. Then they set off again for the Warrs' cottage in the marshes.

Judith opened the door to him. She took one look. 'Hugh – it's all right. Oh, I am so terribly glad.' She flung her arms round him, hugged him and gave him a friendly kiss on the cheek. He would have hugged her back had it not been for the champagne he was clutching. This evening he could cope with anything, even a friendly kiss from Judith.

'What's that?' she demanded. 'Champagne?'

'Champagne? What's this about champagne?' Warr's voice came from the sitting-room. 'Put it on ice,' he added briskly.

'Give it to me, Hugh, I'll see to it,' Judith said.

Hugh went into the book-lined sitting-room, where Warr was lying in a pool of lamplight in front of a log fire, surrounded by sheets of foolscap.

'Are you back on, Hugh?' he asked immediately.

'Yes.'

'That's a relief,' Warr said with satisfaction. 'Pleased?'

'I can't tell you how pleased. I don't know what to do with myself – I feel quite mad.'

Judith came in with champagne glasses.

'Splendid. That's what I like to see,' Warr said. 'Play Hugh something appropriate while the wine cools,' he added, stacking his papers. 'I've done enough work. Come on, Judy, wine, women and song.'

Judith sat down at the great piano reflectively, and then launched triumphantly into some bars from the Academic Festival Overture. Hugh began laughing. 'That sums it up completely,' he said. 'That's exactly how I feel.' He began strutting pompously, until Judith giggled hopelessly and nearly fell off the piano stool. He seized her round the waist, pulled her to her feet, and danced her round the room. Judith broke away, her breath coming fast, and said, 'I'll get the champagne now.'

She brought the bottle in for him to open, and as he was fiddling with the wire he looked across the room to where Colin lay, gaunt and haggard under the lamp, and Judith glowing, as she leant over the back of the chesterfield, looked down at him. He knew then whatever pain it brought him, he was bound to this couple by love and affection for both of them. He poured the champagne.

'Your future,' Colin said seriously, his laughter forgotten. 'This is only the beginning of the road back. You'll make it.'

Jock Calderwood said more or less the same the next day. He insisted on taking Hugh for a celebration lunch. 'Well, now,' he said, as they sat among the Rotarians in the Rose and Crown's gilded restaurant and ate its pretentious tasteless food, 'well, now, we shall have to see about finding you a proper job.'

'Not until we've got Colin's research off,' Hugh said quickly. He paused, and wondered if he meant this.

He was soon put to the test. Archie wrote,

in reply to Hugh's letter telling him the news, offering him a job in the laboratories at Cambridge as a biochemist.

Hugh wrote back thanking him, and saying he could not leave Brookhampton at present. Not until Warr's research was completed, which would take about another six months or so.

Archie wrote back irritably, pointing out that he didn't propose to keep the offer open. This letter was followed by a telephone call from Rodney, who wanted to know if he was out of his mind.

'Oh, I daresay,' Hugh said easily. He could guess what this was about. 'But only nor'-nor'west.'

'I'm talking about the Cambridge biochemistry post,' Rodney said, unamused. 'I don't think you can have grasped how many people are after it. Dad was stretching a point in offering it to you at all.'

'Very good of him,' Hugh said formally. 'But I explained to him that, apart from anything else, I can't leave here at present.'

'But look – I don't want to be brutal, but you've got to face it, Hugh. You aren't in a position to pick and choose. You can't afford to let an opportunity like this slip.'

'I haven't any option.'

'I feel sure Warr would release you if you put it to him. He would know as well as I do that–'

'I'm not going to put it to him.'

'But–'

'There are some things I won't do, and this is one of them.'

'You're throwing your career away a second time, you know that?'

'It's not possible, and that's all there is to it.'

'I'm coming down to see you,' Rodney said.

He turned up on the seven o'clock train that evening, and Hugh took him to the Cliffords' house. If they were going to have a battle, he thought, they had better have it in privacy. Mrs Clifford gave them an excellent meal of lamb chops, chips, peas and tomatoes, followed by apple pie and cups of strong tea. Rodney ate up happily, talking of *Sea Goose*, though he raised his eyebrows when he first saw the room, and again when the tea appeared.

'*Tea*,' he said. 'After *chops*. Most indigestible. The fibres...' He muttered for a while about tannin and meat fibres, and amazed Hugh by his sudden likeness to Archie. However, over the unwelcome tea – which he managed to drink, despite his complaints – he came down to the real issue.

'Now look here,' he began with immense firmness, 'this job. You've got to pull yourself together, and take it seriously.'

'I have taken it seriously. I'm not as unaware of what I'm doing as you seem to imagine.'

'Just because you think you've some sort of obligation towards Warr–'

'I have an obligation. I can't take any job now. I've got one, and I'm sticking to it.'

'I'm sure Warr would advise you to take this other post. He would know that his own research ought to take second place.'

'I agree with you. He would decide exactly that, which is why I don't intend him to know anything about it.'

Rodney frowned. 'There's no pie in the sky, you know, for behaving loyally and unselfishly. No one's going to say "now we must give Hugh Ravelston a reward for being a good boy".'

'I know that. All anyone's going to say is "Hugh Ravelston, who's he?".'

'If you don't look out, that will be it. Look, Hugh, for God's sake take this excellent offer and be thankful.'

'Back to where we came in. No.'

'Warr would only think you a fool. For the Lord's sake show some sense of reality.'

'Expediency, you mean.'

'All right, call it expediency, call it any rude name you like. I don't care what you call it, all I want is for you to do something sensible about your future. You can't throw chances away like this.'

'You can't stop me.'

Rodney sighed. 'I'm not going to stand by watching you go through life making one mistake after another.'

'The situation is more complicated than you allow for,' Hugh said, realising that he owed it to Rodney to explain himself. 'It isn't simply that I won't leave Warr's project at this stage. I hope I wouldn't anyway, no matter what I was offered. But I don't happen to want a career in biochemistry, so the temptation's not overwhelming.'

'You – don't – want–' Rodney let his breath hiss out. 'Listen, half-wit. You'll take what you can get, and be thankful. You can't pick and choose. I'm sorry about it, but there it is. You must face it. It's time you woke up.'

'I know perfectly well there's hardly a chance I'll land the sort of job I want. You don't have to tell me that.'

'Are you under the impression you're going to get back into clinical medicine?'

'I shall try.'

Rodney groaned. 'I was afraid that was it,' he said. 'It's too late, old boy. You'll be banging your head against a brick wall. I won't let you do it.'

'You can't stop me. You can only mop me up afterwards. I shall probably need it.'

'But–'

'I should never be able to look myself in the face if I didn't at least try. Probably it's hopeless, but let me have a bash.'

'That's all very well. But it's out of the question, I'm afraid. The sooner you face it, come to terms with it, the better.'

'I can see as well as you can that clinical medicine is about the most idiotic choice I could make, careerwise, and that I'd better get over the idea, if I can. But I can't. Life, after all, is more than calculation. It's people. It's people I'm interested in. People and diseases, not diseases without people. If I had my choice – and you don't need to jump down my throat and tell me how improbable it is that I shall have any choice in the matter – I'd go in for general medicine. As it is, though, I thought I'd try paediatrics.'

'Now why paediatrics?' Rodney asked. 'I wouldn't have thought it was your line at all.' Hugh Ravelston, looking after sick children? It didn't seem in character. Had he changed as much as this?

'I wouldn't mind spending the rest of my life doing something about children,' Hugh said. He hesitated. He found it almost impossible to explain, even to Rodney. 'You know,' he said eventually, 'on the whole I had a bad childhood. Not materially, of course. But – you know – Annabel was not an easy mother.'

Rodney was startled. This had for years been Hugh's blind spot.

'Well, I see children with far worse difficulties than I ever faced, with physical disabilities that make their lives nothing but a burden, but they struggle on. And half the time they're held back by their parents. Not helped at all. Like this child Sandra. I told you about her. Her mother's hopeless.'

'There's nothing you can do about *that*.'

'Nothing. But I can see it all. I know what's going on. I'm quite prepared to spend all day and every day dealing with children. This is something that's right for me.'

'Well, how are you going to set about it?' Rodney asked bluntly. 'After all, it's no good shutting our eyes, what paediatrician is going to give you a job? With your history? "And what have you been doing for the past two years, since you left the Central, doctor?" eh?'

'That's the snag, of course. But if they're short enough, they may give me a job at some run-down general hospital at the back of beyond – especially if they're running out of Indians, which they're going to do shortly. Failing that, I might land a post in some vast place for sub-normal kids somewhere.'

Rodney frowned. Hugh was right. This was a possibility. He found it almost un-bearable to contemplate. The appalling waste of a brilliant brain.

'Or there's always general practice,' Hugh added.

'General practice.' Rodney paused, trying to gather himself together. 'Look,' he said, 'you may not be the boy wonder, don't think I'm suggesting it. But a mental hospital or general practice, these days, for you – for God's sake, Hugh, you can do better than that, even now. You've got a brain, you'd be frustrated beyond belief. You wouldn't last a year.'

'You're mistaken.'

'*I'm* mistaken. Try and understand, before it's too late, that you may be the one making a mistake. You can't throw away this fascinating opportunity in biochemistry, at Cambridge, for this sort of thing.'

'Afraid so. There it is,' Hugh said, and set his lips.

Rodney could see further argument was useless. But the crazy waste of it horrified him. He could talk of little else for the next few weeks. Both Emma and his colleagues in the research laboratories became very tired of the subject of Hugh Ravelston's career. Rodney even sought out Ben Calderwood, and urged him to stop Hugh being such an idiot.

'Talk some sense into him over Christmas,' he suggested. 'He said he was staying with your family.'

'That's right,' Ben agreed. 'I'm going home for Christmas – first time for five years. Hugh's going to stay with us.'

Before Christmas, Colin Warr was worse. There was no doubt about it. His X-rays

231

were depressing. Hugh discussed the outcome with Calderwood.

'If I could get the research ahead, so that
he could see it completed–' he began.

'Impossible.'

'I'm afraid it is. If I worked on it flat out,
and we engaged a technician, we couldn't
do it in under two months. And that's an
optimistic estimate.'

'Quite. I shouldn't worry about the
project, Hugh. He knows you'll finish it off
for him. It serves its purpose at present. He
has work that absorbs him. How he manages
it, I don't know. I couldn't. But then Colin
has never been any sort of an egoist. It makes
a difference at times like these.'

'Has he told Judith yet?'

'He said he would. He said he'd hoped not
to have to tell her till after Christmas, but
that he couldn't leave it now. That was after
he'd looked at the X-rays, you see.'

'Oh, he saw them, did he?'

'He insisted. Cooper rang me up about it.
He was very distressed. Couldn't see what
to do. Because they speak for themselves.
We thought about trying to switch them,
but we didn't think we'd pull it off.'

'Well, he'd seen the previous lot, so it
would have been very difficult.'

'Exactly. That was the problem.'

'So he knows as well as we do what's
ahead?'

'Yes.' Calderwood swore, fluently and at some length, and with detailed obscenity. 'When I see someone like Colin, and know what life has done to him, I despair of finding any meaning in it.' He sighed. 'When it's necessary, Judith will come and stay with us. I promised Col, and we'll get her there if we have to knock her over the head first.'

'Do you think strong measures will be needed, then?'

'Colin thinks they will. He says she'll go to ground in the cottage, and refuse to leave. He doesn't want her left there alone. I'm mentioning it now so that I can count on your support.'

'Right.'

'Well, we shall have to live through it all soon enough,' Calderwood said. 'No sense in making ourselves miserable in advance. About Christmas – you'll stay a week, won't you? We've masses of room, as you know. I'm not sure when Ben will have to go back, but Margaret will feel very bereft when he does leave. She always hates it, so I rather thought that if you stayed over an extra day or two, it wouldn't be such an empty house for her. How's your mother?'

'She seems to have accepted the idea that she'll see me at Easter instead of Christmas. She's sent detailed instructions about her present, which appears to involve a trip to Asprey's.' Hugh grinned.

'Your mother always did have expensive tastes.'

'Like me, grandfather felt.'

Calderwood's eyes flicked over Hugh. 'Apart from your Alfa-Romeo, and of course you do go in for an expensive line in suits, I wouldn't say you were an ostentatiously expensive young man. Old man leave you any money?' This matter had been the subject of some speculation generally.

'Yes, he did,' Hugh said. 'I didn't expect him to. I thought he'd cut me off with a shilling. But he left me my share, the same as Rodney and Don, and also, as an extra, he left me Harbour Cottage. I was staggered. So was Archie – he was all set to sell it.'

'I don't suppose the old man meant to break with you, you know. I expect he thought he was teaching you a lesson, and then death overtook him. People of that age seem to imagine they're going to live for ever.'

'He never liked me, though, and I was a great disappointment to him – with reason, poor old boy.'

'Yes. But it was your mother he disliked so much. He just took it out on you.'

'That's quite true. I must admit, I can follow the workings of his mind much better now that I've watched Dominic and Sebastian growing up. I feel very much like Grandfather myself when I contemplate them. Very precious young men, they are.'

'You weren't precious when we first knew you.'

'Oh? Well, that's something. I don't think I can have been far off it, though.'

'I've always considered all the Ravelstons gilded,' Calderwood said, with a glint in his eye. 'I thought you were, like most of your family. A little superficial, too. Too much brain, and not enough hard experience. Your cousin Rodney seems to be setting about remedying that in his own way. I would say the present generation aren't too bad a lot, eh? By the way, that brings me to another point. Margaret and I thought you'd probably like Rodney and Emma to come to our Boxing Day party. We'd be very happy to have them.'

'That would be awfully pleasant,' Hugh said, touched. 'How very nice of you to think of it.'

'The more the merrier. That's settled, then. We'll send them an invitation through the post, but you can go ahead and get them lined up.'

Hugh rang Rodney, who accepted the invitation with alacrity. 'That'll be fun,' he said. 'Matter of fact, we're in a bit of a fix over Christmas this year. Have you heard what the parents have gone and done?'

'No, what?'

'Taken themselves off to Majorca. Of all things.'

'But – but–' Hugh spluttered. 'But Aunt Jean's *always* done Christmas.'

'She announced she wasn't going to, and we could make our own plans. I was stunned.' He sounded it still.

'What on earth got into her?'

'Said she was tired of making arrangements.' There was more to it than this, of course, but Jean and Archie had kept her true reasons to themselves. 'I am not going to have Don bringing that abominable girl here for Christmas, and that's that,' she had declared.

The result was that Don brought Nicola to Rodney and Emma, instead. Emma found her a tiresome guest, undeniably charming, and equally undeniably lazy. Rodney, however, enjoyed having her. She hung on his words, and opened her great green eyes admiringly. She had no difficulty in convincing him that it would be an excellent plan for herself and Don to go to the Calderwoods' Boxing Day party.

Rodney telephoned Jock Calderwood about this. He assented genially. He had not the haziest idea who Nicola was, and he forgot to mention the arrangement to anyone until he and Margaret were changing, when he told her.

'What?' she screeched, her hand poised with lipstick as she leant forward at the dressing-table. She swung round accusingly. 'Not *Nicola?* You haven't let him bring that girl *here?*'

'Afraid so,' he said. 'Do we know her?'

Margaret made an exasperated clicking sound. 'Darling,' she said, 'I *told* you at the time. When Jean was staying here. Nicola is *Hugh's* ex-girl-friend. She dropped him when he came down here, and got herself engaged to Don.'

'Oh,' Calderwood said. 'That girl. I'm afraid it never crossed my mind. In that case, what can Rodney be thinking of?'

'The same as you, presumably,' Margaret said with acerbity. 'Something else.'

'Well, we can't stop her coming now.'

'Ben must warn Hugh.'

'I'll mention it to him,' Jock said. He found Ben and told him what had happened.

'That *bloody* girl. She's done it on purpose. All right, I'll warn him. This is what – oh, blast it all.' In his turn, he disappeared in search of Hugh.

'Nicola? Oh, thanks very much, that just makes my evening, I must say. How splendid of Rodney to have thought of bringing her.'

This was more or less what Emma was hissing angrily at Rodney. She came into their bedroom after bathing the children, and found him there changing.

'A perfectly splendid idea of yours, that was,' she said.

'Eh?' Rodney was lost. What on earth was the girl on about?

'How you can be so unfeeling – I thought you were fond of Hugh.'

'Fond of Hugh? Of course I am. What in the world–'

'Rodney,' she said dramatically, flopping down on the bed. 'You don't even know what you've done.'

Rodney thought this was funny. 'I haven't the slightest idea, I'm afraid,' he said in an amused voice, brushing his hair. 'Break it to me, my sweet.'

'Nicola was Hugh's girl-friend first, before she was Don's,' Emma enunciated in a voice of doom.

'Oh, was she? Yes, I had forgotten. Good lord, of course you're right, I took her for a sail once. I *thought* I'd met her somewhere else.' He appeared to be congratulating himself on his feat of memory, and wore a distinctly smug expression which infuriated Emma.

'Oh, *Rodney*,' she said angrily. She wanted to shake him.

'It doesn't matter, does it?' he asked in tones of sweet reason. 'No harm done. Hugh won't mind. He's had hundreds of girl-friends, must be constantly running up against 'em around the countryside. He'll have got over her long ago. He's never said anything to me about her. Storm in a tea cup. Women have no sense of proportion.'

Don drove them down to Brookhampton in the MG he had bought to please Nicola. He was looking forward to doing a little slumming. It would be pleasant to visit Hugh in his provincial retreat, accompanied by Nicola. This was real triumph.

If he had known what was going through Nicola's mind he would have been less sure of himself.

X

Nicola had been genuinely in love with Hugh, and to forsake him had caused her a great deal of pain. She had achieved the break only with a miserable struggle. She knew she cared less for Don than she had done for Hugh, but she forced herself to put his memory behind her. She could not face the thought of giving up the glittering world she loved for a back street in Brook-hampton.

Once she had made her decision she was surprisingly depressed, and when she met Hugh at the Royal Society of Medicine she was thrown into quite as much of a turmoil as he was. She had been prepared to meet him, she had had her charming little speeches all ready, she had been in command of the situation. But afterwards she was not in command of herself. When the lift had borne him upwards, out of her sight, and she had been left with Don, he seemed a pallid and disagreeable version of Hugh. It was Hugh she loved. What a fool she had been. What could she do?

She began to make plans to meet him again. Until now, these had come to nothing. At last they had succeeded. She was excited. Could it all be going to begin all over again? Nostalgically, she arrayed herself in the dress Hugh had bought her, the long shift of blue and green flowers that she had first worn to the Yacht Club dance at East Callant – before, she remembered sadly, life had gone so wrong for him. She longed now to have suffered through the years at his side.

Hugh noticed the dress at once. It had the opposite effect from that intended. Not normally mean or careful with his money, he experienced an uprush of financial resentment. The sight of Nicky turning up with Don, and wearing the dress he himself had bought her, exasperated him. Had the damned girl been prancing round London in it ever since, with everyone but himself?

Never again would he buy any girl an expensive dress. He made no attempt to go forward and greet her, but lost himself in the crowd.

Nicola saw him turn away. She was undisturbed. He was shy of meeting her. But the evening was before them.

She found Ben glowering at her. Well, she knew how to deal with him. He had been glowering at her for years. She smiled charmingly, and spoke soft words. Ben was polite, as he always was.

'Aren't you going to ask me to dance, Ben?' She stepped lightly forward, trustingly – it seemed – straight into his arms. Unwillingly they received her. They danced. He said very little, but when the dance ended she asked for a drink, and he took her to find one.

If he had been anywhere but at home he would have left her flat. But he had been well brought up, and he could no more walk out on her in his own home when she was a guest than he could have pushed her under a bus. He looked round for someone to introduce her to, and planted her firmly on one of the younger of the local G.P.s, who was delighted.

From then on she circulated happily, in her element, and confident that Hugh would emerge from the crowd at any moment. However, it was Don who emerged, and claimed her. This was a disappointment, and she at once said she was tired of dancing. He took her to the bar in the dining-room, and there, talking to Rodney and Ben, was Hugh.

Ben saw her approaching, and typically, scowled. Rodney and Hugh both observed this, and turned round to ascertain the cause. Don and Nicola. Rodney too looked furious – he had already had it broken to him by Ben that he had done the wrong thing in bringing Nicola down.

Nicola, however, ignored all these unwelcoming faces and smiled radiantly at Hugh. 'Here you are at last,' she cooed. 'Lovely to see you,' she paused.

'Lovely to see you,' Hugh cut in. His tones were icy, and both Ben's and Rodney's fury changed to extreme wariness. This was recognisably Hugh on the warpath. 'Merry Christmas,' Hugh added, with a curling lip and an expression of lively and anticipatory enjoyment. 'And to you Don,' he went on. 'I see poor Nicky's still having to wear the dress I bought her – um – must be three years ago. Isn't it about time you lashed out and bought her another?'

Cast off girl-friends and cast off dresses, in fact. Don looked thunderous, but found nothing to say in reply, while Ben and Rodney were clearly amused.

Nicola's poise remained unimpaired. She

was pleased that Hugh remembered the dress, and she rather agreed with his remark. 'Well, it always has been a perfectly beautiful dress,' she said calmly. 'Everyone says so. Aren't you going to dance with me? It's simply ages since we had a dance together.'

'All right,' he agreed. 'Why not?'

Rodney and Ben – and Don, for that matter – were left goggling.

Rodney looked coldly at Don. 'I want to talk to you,' he said unmistakably.

Ben moved off immediately. Ravelston family row about to take place, he could see. He went and informed his father of this, and gave him a brief resumé of the encounter so far. Jock was amused, and also a little relieved, and went off to relate the story to Colin Warr, who was occupying the study sofa.

'The youngest Ravelston appears well able to hold his own,' he announced. 'He is now dancing with his ex-girl-friend – who I must say does him credit as far as looks go. She is a most absurdly lovely child.'

Judith Warr looked startled. This was the first she had heard of Nicola. 'Who is she?' she asked. The men brought her up to date, Calderwood ending with the account of Hugh's remark about Nicola's dress.

Warr began shaking with laughter. 'I see what you mean,' he agreed. 'He doesn't appear to be exactly in need of our assistance. In fact I'd say no reinforcements are required, and the troops can stand down.'

'Have they been standing to?' Judith enquired.

'Battalions of them, my dear,' Warr told her. 'We've all been getting our swords out of hock, ready to support young Hugh in his hour of trial. Obviously totally unnecessary.'

He was right. Hugh and Nicola were dancing together in apparent amiability, though Hugh had made an attempt to carry on the war by demanding, in brittle and off-putting tones, 'I hope you and Don are enjoying yourselves?'

Nicola accomplished her recurrent trick of melting into a man's arms, and remarked thoughtfully, 'I wouldn't exactly say *that*. I don't think Don often enjoys himself.'

This was undeniably true.

'And of course,' Nicola continued – at last she had Hugh where she wanted him – 'of course he isn't a patch on you. I've never enjoyed myself so much as I did with you.' She gave him a speaking look.

'H'mph,' Hugh said, disconcerted. He gave her a Ravelston glance down the nose.

'Oh darling, don't look at me like that,' she immediately squeaked. 'I simply can't bear it if you do. I never could.'

An alarm bell rang clearly throughout Hugh's system. This occasion was proving dangerous in an unforeseen direction. He knew, instantaneously, that the danger was one he could not risk. Run like hell, a voice in his head warned him.

'Of course, Nicky darling,' he said with a kindly smile, 'you and I will always have a very special sort of friendship, won't we?' He watched her face drop with some pleasure, but he dared not stop for breath. 'I shall always remember the fun we had when I was at the Central. It's almost as though we had grown up together, isn't it?' He fixed her with a glare the old man himself couldn't have bettered, and dared her to interrupt. 'I'm so glad we're going to be cousins by marriage,' he said. 'It's splendid that you're going to marry Don.' He gave her another quelling glare.

Nicola knew when she was beaten. 'I am so dreadfully fond of all of you,' she breathed ecstatically.

Hugh grinned irrepressibly. Was she proposing to start on Rodney or Archie next, he wondered? Then he thought of Annabel, and her opinion of the Ravelstons. 'In bunches, Ravelstons are extremely tedious,' he warned her. 'You'll get far too much of us all. Better make Don take you off on your own.' He hoped he was making himself clear, but was unable to resist adding devilishly 'or you'll end up like Jean – cooking for twenty on *Moon Maid* every week-end.' His eyes sparkled at Nicola's unassumed look of horror. That had caught her on the raw. 'Think on it, Nicky dear, and lay your plans accordingly,' he advised her. 'Now I think you need a good stiff drink. The prospect has plainly been a nasty shock to you.' He took her arm lightly and led her back to the dining-room, where there was no sign of Rodney or Ben, only a morose Don, staring into his whisky.

'There you are,' Hugh said affably. 'Here's Nicky. She needs a stiff drink. She's had a nasty jolt.'

'Yes, darling, a very nasty jolt,' Nicola agreed. 'Hugh says before I know where I am I shall find myself cooking for twenty every week-end on board *Moon Maid*. Darling, you won't ever expect me to do that, will you?' She looked lovingly at him and hung on his arm.

'On second thoughts,' Hugh remarked, 'I was wrong. He'd never be prepared to lay out enough hard cash to buy food for that number.' He raised his eyebrows nastily at Don, and left them.

Nicola looked after him with swimming eyes. She had lost him. He had meant more to her than any other man, and like a fool she had let him go deliberately. It had all been a ghastly mistake, but there was no hope for her now. He had made that quite clear. He was no longer interested in her.

Oh well, make the best of a bad job, she

told herself, and hang on to what you can get. This was one method of keeping Hugh in her life, too. In the family. Who knew what the future might hold?

'Let's dance, darling, shall we?' she said to Don. She melted into his arms, and smiled brilliantly up at him, her green eyes liquid with love for Hugh. Don's mouth hardened. His arms tightened round her. Rodney had said a great many uncomplimentary things to him, but somehow he was going to hang on to this girl, marry her, and make a go of it. He supposed he would have to buy her a dress, too.

Meanwhile Rodney had found his way to the study, where Margaret Calderwood was talking to Ambrose Mortimer, the local geriatrician, and another man, whom she introduced as Mr Snelgrove.

'Mr Snelgrove is the Chairman of my Old People's Committee,' she explained.

'And of just about every other committee this side of the county, isn't that so?' Mortimer remarked.

'I wouldn't go as far as that,' Snelgrove replied with good humour. 'But I do seem to sit on a good many, these days.'

Snelgrove, of course, Rodney remembered. Snelgrove and Marshall, the big firm outside Brookhampton manufacturing electrical components. Snelgrove himself looked more like a farmer than businessman. He was a big, sturdy, placid-looking man, probably in his fifties, with thinning sandy hair and a square jaw. He had a straight, kindly expression. Rodney wondered how misleading this might be.

Margaret Calderwood was lamenting the plight of her old people in winter.

'There's so little one can do,' Mortimer agreed. 'And it's worse at this time of the year, of course.'

'The freezing British bedroom is still with us, and it kills off the very young and the very old.' This was Jim Bailey, a local G.P., mounting his hobby horse.

'I read somewhere,' Mortimer said, 'that if you're trying to warm up a patient with hypothermia, central-heating or an electric fire won't get their temperature back to normal for twenty-four hours, while a hot bath or a coal fire will do it in three or four. Have you struck that?'

'Well, I firmly believe it,' Bailey said. 'But I must admit I've no idea how to prove it.'

Jock Calderwood had been listening, and he chuckled. 'Rodney will turn pale with horror if you go on like that, Jim,' he said. 'You're talking, you know, to a physiologist with almost a corner in hypothermia.' They hadn't, of course, known, as they had none of them – in true British fashion – paid attention to Margaret Calderwood's introduction. 'And just back from the Antarctic, at that,' Calderwood added.

'Oh dear, I feel very silly,' Jim Bailey said. 'Why didn't someone warn me?'

'Most of it is unproven,' Rodney said benignly, though this was not his personal opinion.

'Anyway, what do you consider the most effective method of rewarming?' Mortimer asked. 'While we have the expert here, let's make use of him,' he added to Jim Bailey.

'Hot bath, if you can,' Rodney said confidently. 'Failing that,' he went into details. 'In mountaineering, you know, they've found...' he gave instances. 'Then in the enquiry into the Lakonia disaster, it was felt...'

This was the sort of medical conversation Daniel Snelgrove enjoyed, and he listened avidly. For these moments he tolerated all the hard committee work. He manoeuvred Rodney into a corner, and cross-examined him about the Antarctic. He was an intelligent listener, and Rodney – who could do this if he wanted to – expanded on his experiences, some of which were hair-raising.

Rodney was mellowed by drink, he had already had a very satisfactory row with Don, and he was recognisably the man of action, rather than the backroom scientist his father appeared. He was exactly the type of man Daniel Snelgrove liked. He determined to keep in touch with him, and, as a preliminary, asked Rodney if he would consider giving a talk to the Brookhampton Rotarians. Rodney had had to lecture all over the States the previous year to raise money for the funds, and he had had enough. But Hugh could undoubtedly do with Daniel Snelgrove's backing, if he was going to try for a local post. He accepted the invitation with apparent alacrity.

Calderwood, who had a gift for unobtrusive organisation, saw the diaries come out, and knew his objective had been achieved. Time to move Snelgrove on. He did this, giving him to Colin Warr, who was an old friend.

Rodney began telling Calderwood about the post in Cambridge Hugh had turned down. 'He simply can't be allowed to go on throwing his career down the drain like this,' he urged.

'This is the first I've heard of it,' Calderwood said slowly.

'He's playing with some dreary plan for going into a hospital for mentally subnormal children. I ask you, turning down this Cambridge offer for that.'

'Oh, we can't let him do that,' Calderwood agreed. 'But I must say, I wouldn't have thought very highly of him if he had just pushed off, and left Colin Warr at this juncture.' He explained the situation to Rodney.

'No,' Rodney admitted. 'Of course I see

that now. I didn't at the time. He didn't tell me the poor fellow was dying. Simply said he must finish the research project, and I really couldn't for the life of me see why Warr couldn't perfectly well organise his own research. But as you say, this is a different situation.'

'He'll have to finish the research off and write the paper, you know.'

'I see.'

'I saw this coming some time ago. I hoped it wouldn't materialise, but I knew it might. Colin is very lucky to have Hugh now. But when he took him on, it wasn't so. Hugh was very lucky Colin was prepared to try him out.'

'I see.'

'The project's financed by a fund controlled by Daniel Snelgrove.'

Rodney grinned. 'I rather gain the impression that most local activities are controlled by Daniel Snelgrove, one way or another,' he remarked.

'Quite so. I was glad to see you having a chat with him just now. With regard to Warr, Daniel's completely in the picture, and he's prepared to finance Hugh while he completes the project and writes it up, senior registrar level, we thought.'

'So Hugh won't be available until the summer.'

'No,' Calderwood said doubtfully. 'If you

put it like that, no.'

'I might be able to talk some sense into them at the Central by then,' Rodney pondered. 'I don't see why he shouldn't go into the research labs. They'll never have him on the clinical side, we know that. But – damn it, we need him to crew *Opening Snap*, if for nothing else.' He grinned, and suddenly looked much younger. 'The boat's done hopelessly the last couple of years,' he said. 'I was in the Antarctic, Hugh was down here, and they didn't even have Ben, because he kept disappearing at crucial moments to come down here and sail *Sea Goose* with Hugh.' He laughed. 'My name was mud in the Sailing Club. They said I'd effectively removed three crew members at once. I must point out in the right quarters that if they appoint Hugh to a decent post again they'll automatically get them all back.'

Calderwood chuckled. 'That might have considerable effect, though less than it would have had in your grandfather's day.'

'True.'

'But you know, Hugh is set on clinical medicine.'

'He'll have to get over it,' Rodney said flatly. 'There isn't a career in it any longer for him. It's regrettable, but the sooner he's used to it the better.'

'There isn't a career in the Central,' Calderwood said dubiously. 'But–'

'Can you get him a job here?' Rodney asked quickly.

'I think so.'

'H'm. Better than nothing, of course. But – but he'll never reach the top, will he? With your help, perhaps he can do what he thinks he wants to do, and practise medicine again. Can you land him a consultant post here?'

'I think we might manage it, in due course.'

In due course. When he's going grey, and he's lost half a dozen posts because of his history, they'll decide they perhaps know him well enough to overlook it, and they'll make him the junior consultant in geriatrics, as a concession and provided he does all the dirty work.'

'Not quite as bad as that, I hope. But at least five years, it would take.'

'It's not good enough,' Rodney said decidedly. 'If he'd stayed at the Central he'd have had a Chair of Medicine somewhere or other in his mid-thirties. He'd have been on the staff as a physician in a year or two. Well, that's all gone. He must face it. He's blotted his copybook and they'll never forget it as long as he's dealing with patients. In clinical medicine he'll never achieve more than a second-rate job. He must try to take the long view. In biochemistry it'll be different. No one will give a damn what the G.M.C. once said. He can do some worthwhile research, have some study leave, go to the States on a fellowship – whatever he likes. He's the sort who might pull something out of the hat one day. Open up a new field – biochemistry's wide open. A major discovery. Nobel Prize.'

'Come, come, you're letting your imagination run away with you,' Calderwood suggested, amused.

'Not necessarily. Anyway, Hugh has a brain, and as time goes on, he's going to be damnably frustrated if he can't use it. I admit I find it hard to understand why he's so set on clinical medicine. He'll only be able to do it in a junior capacity. I can't see why he doesn't find the prospect of being able to do some original work vastly more stimulating.'

'But he doesn't, Calderwood retorted. 'You and I don't understand this attitude of his, because neither of us is a clinician. Colin Warr is. He's discussed this with Hugh a good deal. He says Hugh ought to get back to the wards.'

They looked blankly at one another now, a little out of their depth. Both Jock Calderwood and Rodney Ravelston were men whose real homes were their laboratories. They not only felt comfortable as soon as they set foot in them, but they found it hard to grasp that others were unable to share these reactions. Their laboratories were at one and the same time snug and exciting – as restful as old shoes and as stimulating as the base for any exploration into the unknown can be.

'If I thought there was any chance whatsoever that he would succeed,' Rodney said, 'it wouldn't matter a damn whether I understood his motives or not. I'd help him to get where he wanted. But the trouble is, he'll live to regret it. I can see it coming so clearly. He'll watch his juniors pass him, people whose abilities he knows are below his landing the jobs, while he's never even shortlisted, his path blocked. Then he'll know his mistake. He'll be frustrated and embittered, his mind going to seed, his brain wasted. It won't be good for him.'

'You may well be right there,' Calderwood admitted. 'But let's go and talk to Col. He's the one who's in favour of him being a clinician in spite of everything. And he's a realistic sort of chap.'

They joined the group round the sofa, where Taylor and Snelgrove were talking to Warr.

'This is Hugh's cousin, Rodney Ravelston,' Calderwood began.

'Ah, the physiologist,' Warr said, smiling widely, his eyes alight with amusement. He had been told already about Jim Bailey's embarrassment. 'And the owner of *Sea Goose*,' he added. 'I must thank you for some extremely pleasant sailing we had this year.'

'Oh, I'm glad,' Rodney said. This was true. He found himself delighted beyond all reason to have been in any way instrumental in helping Colin Warr during his last summer. He knew, too, why Hugh could have done nothing but turn down the Cambridge job. All this in the flicker of their eyes meeting, and the sense of Warr's unquenchable spirit. They began talking. Between them they mapped out Hugh's future.

Some time later, Calderwood returned to the study to find Warr, Taylor and Snelgrove talking about the Ravelstons.

'Handsome family, aren't they?' Colin Warr was saying.

'And here in force tonight,' Taylor added, amused.

'Oh, this is only the younger generation,' Calderwood remarked. 'If you'd been trained at the Central, you'd understand the meaning of the Ravelstons in force. Of course, the old boy was alive then.'

'Sir Donald Ravelston?' Taylor asked.

'Yes – he was these boys' grandfather. Then there's Professor A.D.R. Ravelston – the physiologist.'

'The heart muscle man?'

'That's right. He's Rodney's father.'

'Eminent medical circles Hugh moved in before he came down here,' Warr commented, watching Taylor.

'Have they *all* that look of hauteur?' Taylor asked.

'The old man had it to excess – what you've seen tonight is a milder version by far. In fact, I think it's mainly something to do with the formation of the nose.'

'They're an interesting family, aren't they? If we can entice one on the staff here, I think we'd be doing quite well,' Snelgrove suggested. He was, needless to say, Chairman of the Brookhampton Hospital Management Committee.

'I agree. We've got him, we want to hang on to him. I don't suppose we'll be able to keep him long, though,' Calderwood added, his eyes also on Taylor.

'No? He has his – so to speak – disability,' Taylor said.

'He's already been offered a post at Cambridge,' Calderwood remarked. 'But he's turned it down.'

'What's that?' Warr demanded sharply. 'Why wasn't I told?'

'I only heard this evening,' Calderwood explained. 'Rodney told me.'

'He didn't tell *me.*'

'Apparently he came down here and tried to talk him round, but Hugh wouldn't budge.'

'Why not?'

'Said he was going to finish your research.'

'Damned young fool. I'd have let him go.'

'I'd have been bloody annoyed with him if he hadn't turned it down,' Calderwood said.

'We must think of his future,' Warr argued.

'He'll have plenty of offers,' Calderwood said. 'Rodney thinks they'll want him at the Central Research Labs. He foresees a Nobel Prize – but that may possibly have been due to my whisky.'

'A Nobel Prize,' Snelgrove repeated, impressed.

'Alcoholic exuberance,' Calderwood explained with a grin.

'I wouldn't be surprised if one of the Ravelstons didn't land one,' Warr suggested.

'Well, it won't be Hugh, if he goes back to clinical medicine,' Calderwood pointed out.

'He's a born clinician,' Warr said.

'No one's a born anything,' Calderwood retorted. 'He'll go much further in biochemistry.'

'If he wants to be a clinician, I think we should encourage him,' Taylor said. 'While we have the chance, eh? I'd have him as my registrar like a shot. Damned lucky to get him.'

Warr and Calderwood exchanged a glance.

'You'd find him good, I think,' Warr said cautiously.

'That would be a relief,' Taylor said. 'I haven't had a good registrar since young David Wargrave packed it in and went to Australia.'

Later Warr and Calderwood exchanged winks. 'I think, you know, we've pulled it off,' Warr said.

'They're both sold on the idea,' Calderwood agreed.

'You old manager – I leave his future in your capable hands. All I hope is that Taylor doesn't turn huffy when he finds his registrar's more able than he is himself.'

'Hugh will have to be tactful. He'd better get used to knowing more than his seniors and concealing it from them, because life will be like that for a long, long time. Rodney may be right when he urges him to go into biochemistry, you know. Frustration and being passed over is bad for anyone.'

'He'll have to decide for himself,' Warr said. 'It's up to him.' He was exhausted. But he had a sense of achievement. He had done all it was in his power to do, had made provision for what mattered to him – Judith's future, his own research project, Hugh Ravelston's career. He was very tired, and he had had enough of fighting. Now he could let go.

XI

Hugh was dancing with Judith. He felt he needed to hold on to her. She was looking very lovely, this evening, though exhausted and pale. Her eyes were sunk deeply into their sockets, and shadowed with a delicate purple that came out of no make-up box, and the bones of her face showed their beauty. She was wearing a classic dress of golden yellow velvet, with an amber necklace and ear drops that matched her hair – scooped back from her wide forehead into a low knot on the nape of her neck.

She adopted Colin's tactics of plunging straight into the conversation. 'Where,' she asked at once, 'is this girl-friend of yours that everyone's talking about?'

Hugh was taken aback, and his face showed it. 'Over there,' he answered in a flattened voice. 'In the straight dress with the swirling pattern in blue and green.'

'Well, of course, she's absolutely lovely, as they all said,' Judith admitted.

'She is very decorative,' he said in neutral tones.

'Oh, for heaven's sake, Hugh, come off it. If you don't want to talk about her, say so, but don't use that voice at me.'

He sighed. 'If I knew what I wanted to say about her I'd say it.'

'Begin at the beginning. I never heard a word about her until tonight, though Col seems to be in the picture. Were you very much in love with her?'

'I thought I was.'

'You *thought* you were? You mean you think you aren't now?'

'I know I'm not now,' he said firmly. With Judith in his arms, he could be sure of this at least.'

'What happened?'

'She left me and took up with my cousin Don – she's dancing with him now.'

'Did she drop you because you weren't a success any more?' she asked baldly.

'At the time that's what I thought.'

'She sounds a thoroughly disagreeable girl. I'm sure you're well rid of her, however much it hurt you at the time. If you were thinking of marrying her–'

'I was then.'

'It's just as well you found out in time.'

'Yes. She's lovely, but trivial. I see that now. Besides you, for instance, she's trivial.'

Judith gave him a serious look, as if to assess his sincerity. Then she said, 'Life has stopped me being trivial.'

'I don't believe you ever were.'

She looked at him again, straight in the

eyes. 'Colin matured me a great deal,' she said. 'Before I met him I was a much shallower person. Beside him, you know, I'm still almost infantile.'

He held her tightly, and they danced in silence for some minutes. Suddenly she burst out, 'If only I had known earlier about Colin. All those months of him I wasted. Why didn't you tell me?'

'He didn't want you to be told.'

'I asked you, and you lied.'

'Colin wanted you to have peace of mind.'

'Colin wanted – Colin wanted. Why didn't you think of me? What sort of price have I paid for peace of mind? What price did Colin pay at the time? Knowing he was dying, and never able to share his feelings with me? Carrying on alone.'

'It was for him to decide, I thought.'

'You could have taken matters into your own hands, and told me.'

'I'm sorry, I didn't feel I could.'

'No, you're right, of course you couldn't,' she said fairly. 'You weren't in a position to. But Jock could have told me. Somebody could have told me.'

This was an agonising thrust. To be written off in this way was a thousand times more painful than to be blamed for her unhappiness. He could see she was unconscious of having wounded him, and his heart twisted with a strange jealousy and misery. All he said was 'no one liked to.'

She raised her eyes then, filled with more pain than he could bear. But he didn't have to bear it, he thought, she did. There was nothing he could do about it. There was silence between them.

Suddenly she exclaimed, 'All of you have been treating me like a child. Who had to be spared any unpleasantness.'

'I don't think–'

'Col has always treated me more like a daughter than a wife,' she muttered. She flushed. 'I've never told anyone that before. You must forget it. He's meant it for the best, and it's partly his nature. But I wanted to be more than that to him. Our life could have been so different if only he could have accepted me as an equal. I always thought one day he would. Now it's too late. It's never going to happen. But I wanted to be some use to him.'

'I'm sure you–'

'Cooking a few meals and running the house,' she said scornfully. 'That's not what I'm talking about. *You've* been more help to him than I have. Or Jock. And you've all been conspiring with him, to spare me any pain. What do you all think I am?'

'Judy–'

'I know. You needn't tell me. A childish egotist. That's what I sound like. Colin's dying, and all I can talk about is me, and my feelings. But I'm being truthful with you. I can't say any of this to Colin, I'm not quite as selfish as that, I can't turn round and grumble at him that he hasn't given me a chance to show what I'm made of, when he's dying. But I've got to let it out to someone, all these things I'm thinking.'

He said nothing, tried to will reassurance to flow from his hands into her.

'What you've all done,' she said, 'is to prevent me from knowing the truth, and somehow – I don't know how, I haven't had the chance to find out – somehow growing with it. My last opportunity to be a real wife to Colin, taken away from me.' She looked at him with despair in her eyes. 'What am I going to do without him?' she asked. 'How can I possibly live without him?' She searched his features, as if there might be an answer to be read there.

'Try not to be sad while you still have him,' Hugh said. He was taut with the pain of what seemed to him to be her rejection of any support but Colin's. Only Colin existed for her. He must bear this knowledge without a sign.

'You're right,' she was saying. 'Oh, Hugh, you're absolutely right. I mustn't be miserable yet.'

'Don't keep having rehearsals,' he suggested.

'No rehearsals,' she agreed. Her body

went limp in his steadying arms, and she rested her head momentarily against his shoulder. He longed to cradle it, to murmur his love, to bring her relief. But he knew there was nothing he could do.

In February Colin was admitted again, for what was to be his last illness. He had a third course of radiotherapy, which was discontinued when he failed to respond. The treatment left him very weak, and his condition began to deteriorate rapidly. They all knew he was dying.

His breathing was difficult, and he could speak only in brief phrases. Soon he was under heavy sedation, and began to wander in thought, though now and again he was as alert and coherent as he had ever been.

During one of these lucid intervals he told Hugh, who was sitting with him while Judith had her supper, that he had written a letter to be given to her after his death. Hugh would find it, he said, in his desk, in the right-hand drawer.

'I wanted her,' he paused, 'to have it in writing. Don't want her – imagining – a lot of nonsense – afterwards.' He seemed to think he had explained everything, and lapsed into silence. Hugh wondered what he was talking about, but decided that as it was evidently in the letter, there was no need to rouse him to enquire. But Warr roused himself.

'Don't understand, do you?' he asked.

'No.'

'Told her – marry again.' He opened his eyes suddenly and caught Hugh's glance. 'Don't look so upset,' he said. 'You marry her. Best thing.'

'She may not want me to.'

He smiled gently. 'She will. If you go after her. Want to?'

'Yes. But–'

'Then go and get her.'

'I don't think–' Hugh looked helplessly at Colin.

'What?'

'I don't feel I'd be much good to a girl who's had you for a husband.' This was the truth, though he found it hard to admit, even to Colin, even now.

'Don't be humble. Doesn't suit you.'

'Uncharacteristic, no doubt.'

Colin smiled. 'Highly. And uncalled for.' He lay breathing shallowly for some minutes, then roused himself. 'What's wrong with you,' he said, 'is that you've woken up – to find – you're no great improvement – on anyone else.' He paused again. 'Doesn't matter,' he said. 'Good enough.'

'I daresay it'll have to be,' Hugh agreed. It was like Colin, he thought, to have found the strength as his life was ebbing to make it possible for him to seek Judith's love.

He died the next day – a gusty April day, with the trees whipping in the wind as Hugh drove Judith across the marshes to the Calderwoods, and the spears of spring rain cooling his bare head as he walked the roads afterwards in desolation and sorrow.

As spring moved towards uncertain summer, he helped Judith to pack up the cottage. She was leaving Brookhampton to teach at a summer school in the United States, a trip arranged for her by an anxious friend in London.

'It's just the thing for you,' Hugh said, when she told him. 'You must accept at once.'

'But I don't want to go.'

'Don't be silly,' he said brusquely.

'I want to stay here.'

'What would Col say?'

She sniffed, and blew her nose. 'Both of you,' she muttered, 'always making me *do* things.'

Hugh had found Colin's letter to her, in his desk, as he had said it would be. He gave it to her. She read it, and passed it back to him.

The letter was brief, and unemotional.

When you have been ill for as long as I have now, death can come as a relief. I am tired, and I have nearly had enough. So don't grieve too much. This is for you after I've gone. I am sorry to be leaving you on your own. Remember I love you, and try not to be sad. Life is for the living, and you must share yours with someone. This is what I want for you. Never forget that. I am sorry that first of all you will have to face a difficult and lonely time, but there is no way out for either of us.

'No way out,' Judith repeated, her face wet with tears.

'None,' Hugh agreed. 'You have to live through your bad time now.' He paused, thinking of Colin Warr as he had so often sat, slumped on a stool in the laboratory, looking at the results of innumerable tests and talking about life. 'I shall never forget Colin,' he said, thinking aloud. 'He taught me how to grow up.'

'I shall have to do that without him,' Judith said wanly. 'All by myself in Michigan. All those new places, that I used to want to see, and I shall simply be thinking of Colin.' Her lips were quivering, and her voice husky with tears.

'Think of me too,' Hugh said firmly.

'I'd rather stay here. I don't want to go away at all.' She looked about her, and spread her hands despairingly. 'So much has happened in this room – I can't go away and leave it. I want to stay here and reflect on it all, sort it all out.' She passed her hand tenderly along Colin's desk, and moved to shake the cushions on the chesterfield. She looked down as if she saw Colin himself lying there. 'Do you remember,' she asked, 'that evening when you came with champagne? And I played the

Academic Festival Overture for you? I tried to be glad about your news – and in a way I was, of course – but secretly I was sorry, because I knew you'd be going out of my life. That's what I thought. But it was Colin who went, not you.' She took his hand and held it tightly, desperately.

'Not me, no,' Hugh agreed. 'I shall always be around, if you want me. Remember that.'

He went to London Airport on a warm June evening to see her off. She had lost weight, and looked fragile and a little pale, only her glorious hair catching the last of the sunlight and glowing with brilliant copper. She wore a plain black linen sleeveless dress, and carried a battered old music case bulging with scores. He saw her suddenly as young and very vulnerable.

'I'll be waiting for you here,' he said, and hugged her.

'Oh yes,' she said vehemently, clinging to him with sudden anguish. 'Please be waiting for me. And write to me.' Then there was no more time. She had to board the plane. He stood watching while it took off, circled the summer sky, and disappeared into the sunset.

Then he turned on his heel, and made for the underground. He had to return to Brookhampton that night, to be in time for medical outpatients the next morning. He was lonely, but full of hope.

The publishers hope that this book has given you enjoyable reading. Large Print Books are especially designed to be as easy to see and hold as possible. If you wish a complete list of our books please ask at your local library or write directly to:

Dales Large Print Books
Magna House, Long Preston,
Skipton, North Yorkshire.
BD23 4ND

This Large Print Book, for people
who cannot read normal print,
is published under the auspices of

THE ULVERSCROFT FOUNDATION